LORD FREDDIE'S KISS

"What a marvelous present for your sister," Anne said, still not taking her eyes from the fireworks in the sky.

"It was nothing," Freddie said. "Priscilla has been begging me for the last year to take her to Vauxhall Gardens, to see the illuminations. But Vauxhall Gardens is not the safest of places for an impressionable girl. So instead I brought the fireworks to her."

"You are the best of brothers," Anne said.

The word "brother" scraped against his nerve endings. He did not want her to admire him for his kindness. He did not want her to see him as simply a good brother. He did not even want to be her friend.

"Come," he said, taking her by the arm. Freddie pulled her away from the steps, into the shrubbery where the shadows were thickest.

Letting go of her arm, Freddie turned to face her. He cupped her face between his hands. Time seemed to stop for a moment, and then he bent his head down and his lips brushed hers. Her lips were soft and warm beneath his. He drew his head back for a moment and saw the surprise in her eyes, the flush in her cheeks.

He dropped his hands down and took her hands in his. He raised them to his lips, kissed first the left and then the right. Then he placed her hands on his shoulders and drew her into his embrace. . . .

Books by Patricia Bray

A LONDON SEASON
AN UNLIKELY ALLIANCE
LORD FREDDIE'S FIRST LOVE

Published by Zebra Books

LORD FREDDIE'S FIRST LOVE

Patricia Bray

Zebra Books
Kensington Publishing Corp.

http://www.zebrabooks.com

ZEBRA BOOKS are published by

Kensington Publishing Corp.
850 Third Avenue
New York, NY 10022

First Printing: September, 1999
10 9 8 7 6 5 4 3 2 1

Printed in the United States of America

One

George Harold Arthur Pennington, sixth Viscount Frederick, known to his closest friends as Freddie, clasped Miss Sommersby's dainty gloved hand between his own. Taking a deep breath, he said, "And so, Miss Sommersby, having told you of my admiration and esteem for you, and daring to hope that you feel the same toward me, I ask your permission to speak with your father to secure his permission for our marriage."

The incomparable Miss Sommersby blinked her celestial blue eyes. "Oh, dear," she said, withdrawing her hand from his. "I never expected this."

There was a sinking feeling in his chest. A less experienced gentleman might have taken her words for maidenly modesty, but after twelve marriage proposals Lord Frederick knew better. "You must have had some inkling of my intentions, if not over these past weeks, then certainly you must have known why I requested a private audience with you," he said, feeling that he deserved at least some explanation. After all, he had squired Miss Sommersby around London for the last two months. And though she had admirers in plenty, Lord Frederick had been her most constant escort, until by now all of London was expecting an announcement.

"Oh, dear," Miss Sommersby repeated. Her porcelain brow wrinkled in thought. "I realize how it must have appeared, but in truth it never occurred to me that your attentions might be serious."

He had been courting the girl for weeks now, and she hadn't even noticed. It was mortifying. He hoped frantically that no one was listening at the door. If word of this got out, he would be a laughingstock.

"You must forgive my presumption," he said, suddenly anxious to leave.

But Miss Sommersby was not prepared to let him escape unscathed. "I do hope you are not terribly devastated," she said. "I am sensible of the great honor you do me, but I can not accept for I have already met my one true soul mate."

"Who?" he asked, curious in spite of himself. He could not recall her paying special attention to any one of her suitors. Indeed she had shown a marked preference for his company. It was this that had led him to hope he had finally found a woman to be his wife.

"Edward Farquhar," she said, with a delicate blush.

"Hmmm. I take it your family does not approve?" He did not blame them. Edward Farquhar was a dirty dish, with a bad habit of courting naive heiresses. His only redeeming grace was that he was always willing to break off his courtships, provided the girl's family paid him handsomely. Indulgent papas took one look at Edward Farquhar and gladly paid to be rid of him. Farquhar would have been drummed out of Society long ago, if not for his cousin the Duke of Aylsworth.

Her features took on a petulant cast. "No, and they are being positively medieval over the matter. They claim that Edward is a rake and a fortune hunter, and have forbidden me to see him."

"Farquhar does have a certain reputation," he said, though from the starry light in her eyes, he knew it was no use warning her.

She waved her hand dismissively. "He has renounced his rakish ways," she declared. "When we first met we knew at once that we were soul mates. Edward said that my love has saved him from his dark side. He has changed, though my parents refuse to accept this. They try to keep us apart, but a love like ours will not be denied."

He looked at her and wondered how he could ever have contemplated marriage to her. Miss Sommersby was so young, so dreadfully young and naive. And there was nothing he could do to save her from herself. She would have to discover Farquhar's perfidy in her own time.

"I wish you every happiness," he said at last. And he truly meant it, despite the blow she had dealt to his pride.

"You are most kind. And please, I hope that the three of us can be friends. I know you will like Edward, and I would hate to lose your friendship. I have always thought of you as the brother I never had."

A brother. He wondered what she would think if he pulled her into his arms and pressed heated kisses onto her shell pink lips. Was that what it would take to make her see him as a man? If so, he would never know, for he had too much honor in him to take advantage of an innocent.

He asked her to convey his regards to her parents, and after assuring her for the tenth time that his heart was not broken, he was finally able to escape with what little remained of his dignity.

His carriage was waiting outside, but he dismissed it, preferring to walk instead. He wanted the time to think. Miss Sommersby had wounded his pride, if not his heart. A brother. The incomparable Miss Sommersby, one of the reigning toasts of the Season, thought of him as a brother.

Her remark had cut to the quick, more so because he had heard it more times than he cared to remember. Over the years he had proposed marriage to thirteen women. The first had been Anne Webster, the daughter of a neighboring family. He had been just seventeen and Anne fifteen when he had proposed. He had been sincere in his offer, but Anne had refused, rightly pointing out that they were both too young. At least she hadn't said that her affection for him was sisterly in nature.

Since then he had proposed marriage a dozen more times. The awkward boyish stammer of his first proposal had given way to the polished addresses of a London gentleman. The results were still the same. Each lady had declined the honor of becoming his wife, and after Anne, each had managed to use the word brother while doing so.

He had pinned his hopes on Miss Sommersby. True, she was young, but at seven and twenty he was not precisely ancient himself. He had enjoyed the time he spent in her company, and would have sworn that she felt the same.

She had seemed such a sensible girl. A trifle young to be a viscountess, but with his mother still in residence at Beechwood Park, there would be time for her to grow into her responsibilities. So he had offered her a marriage based on mutual respect and friendship.

And she had declined, preferring to throw herself away on a loose screw like Edward Farquhar. But women were like that. A worthy gentleman was declared a dull bore, while a rake like Farquhar could have any woman he wanted.

Of course there were plenty of women who would have jumped at the chance to become Viscountess Frederick. Women who looked at him and saw a respectable title and a set of prosperous estates. They would have pursued him had he been an ancient lecher or a mumbling idiot. Was it so wrong of him to want more in a marriage? He no longer sought romantic love, but was it asking too much that he find one woman who could be both friend and wife?

Now he was feeling sorry for himself. And he despised self-pity. Miss Sommersby's rejection was not the end of the world. He was still young. There was plenty of time for him to find a wife. He would just have to go about his search more carefully this time. He scowled down at the sidewalk, wondering how much gossip there would be when it became clear that Miss Sommersby had refused the honor of becoming the next Viscountess Frederick.

"Freddie! Have you gone deaf?"

He turned and saw that his friend Lord Glendale had pulled a curricle alongside.

"Returning home?" Glendale asked.

Freddie nodded.

"I was coming to see you anyway. Climb in, and I will save you the trouble of walking."

He did not feel like company, but he could hardly snub his oldest friend. "Very well," he said.

Glendale moved over, and Freddie climbed up onto the seat beside him.

His friend started the horses with a flick of the whip, weaving them expertly in and out of the confusion that was characteristic of a London morning.

"Why the long face?"

Freddie sighed. "Miss Sommersby."

"I see," Glendale said. As his closest friend, he needed no other explanation. "I am sorry. I know how fond you were of her."

"And she was fond of me as well. As a brother," Freddie said, with a creditable attempt at a laugh.

"I am sorry," Glendale repeated. Mercifully he fell silent. He did not attempt to console Freddie by pointing out all the reasons why Miss Sommersby had been wrong for him. Nor did he reassure Freddie that there were plenty of ladies who would eagerly become his wife. With the rapport that comes from long friendship he seemed to realize that Freddie knew all those things already. Instead he gave Freddie his silence and support.

Freddie shook himself out of his doldrums. "You mentioned you were coming to see me?"

"Yes," Glendale said. He glanced over at Freddie, then seemed to come to a decision. "Jane and I have decided to leave London earlier than planned. We'll be departing for the country on Friday. I know you were set to join us after the Season, but you are more than welcome to travel with us now. And your sister Priscilla as well."

"Priscilla has gone to stay with our sister Elizabeth," Freddie said. "But why the haste? I thought you fixed in London for at least another month." A chance to escape the London gossip seemed heaven-sent. Freddie couldn't help wondering if Glendale had realized this and moved forward the trip to the countryside.

"This is confidential, mind you, but Jane announced this morning that she is expecting our child. And nothing will do for her but to leave London at once and go home to Stonefield." Glendale grinned with obvious pleasure.

"You lucky devil! Congratulations!" Freddie said, thumping his friend on the back. And he meant it. He really did. Despite the stab of envy as he realized that here, too, his friend had surpassed him. Not only had Glendale found a wife who adored him, now he was to start a family of his own.

"But you will want to be alone," Freddie said. "You do not need my company."

"On the contrary," his friend replied. "The boys are in school for another month, but Jane's mother and her sisters are already in residence. I will be veritably outnumbered by the female contingent, and I am counting on you to save my sanity."

"Thank you, but no," Freddie said. If it had been just Jane and Glendale he might have been tempted. But knowing that her five sisters would be there was too much. At least two of her sisters were of marriageable age; still, they had all developed the habit of calling him Uncle Freddie. He had never before minded. Until now.

Glendale urged him to reconsider, but he remained firm. He pleaded urgent business at home that could not be put off. He doubted that Glendale believed the story, but his friend was kind enough not to call him a liar. Instead Glendale insisted that Freddie was welcome to join them whenever his business was concluded, and Freddie promised to do that.

"Are we there yet?" Ian asked, leaning forward on the carriage seat to peer out the window.

"Soon, precious," Anne Webster replied. The carriage swayed as it hit a rut, and reaching over she caught hold of his jacket as he started to fall. "Be a good boy, and sit back on the seat like a proper gentleman. You can still see out the window from here."

"Yes, Mama," Ian promised, but within moments he was leaning forward again, his head stuck out the open window to better see the countryside.

Anne sighed. Ian was a good lad, really he was. But he was also a bundle of energy in the way that only six-year-olds can manage. After weeks of travel, the effort of keeping Ian out of mischief was beginning to show. If only Nurse had been well enough to accompany them. But Mrs. Flinders, good woman that she was, had not been willing to make the long Atlantic voyage.

And the maid Anne had hired had proved a disaster. The girl had shirked her duties for the entire voyage, then had disappeared as soon as the ship docked in England. Rather than trying to find another maid, Anne had decided to simply press on to New Biddeford.

To be honest, it was not simply the strain of travel

and of watching over Ian that kept her awake nights. She had taken care of Ian with no help before, and was perfectly capable of seeing to his needs. In truth, it was that she did not want this journey to end. The closer she came to her childhood home, the more she dreaded her arrival. For despite her father's summons, she held little hope that her reception would be anything other than frosty. She wondered for the hundredth time why he had finally decided to send for them after ignoring their existence for all these years.

"Now, remember what I told you? We are here to see my papa, but he is very old and we must make allowances if he seems gruff and unfriendly."

"I promise not to trouble him," Ian said obediently.

"It will only be a short visit," Anne said, trying to comfort herself as well as Ian.

Ian twisted around to look at her. "This was your home, Mama? When you were little?"

"Yes," she said.

"But it is not your home anymore?"

It was too much for her to explain to a child. Especially to Ian, who was an innocent in all this. "My home is with you," she said finally. "We will see my papa, and then we will return to New Halifax, and everything will be as it was before."

Ian nodded gravely, his hazel eyes serious. In that moment he looked far older than his years. "Don't worry, Mama," he said. "If your papa doesn't want you, then I will take care of you."

She felt a stab of guilt. Ian knew far too much about rejection. She vowed furiously that she would protect him, come what may. If her father said one unkind word, she would take Ian and leave at once.

They came upon the village of New Biddeford. Glancing out the window, she was struck by how little had changed in the years she had been absent. The church, the village green, even the shops looked untouched by time. Save for the new sign on the posting house, it might have been only yesterday that she had left.

It was all so familiar, yet at the same time everything seemed older and more imposing than she had remembered. Compared to the raw newness that was so much of Canada, the village had a feel of history, of endless generations. The buildings themselves seemed to remember her. And to judge her. It was a strange thought, and she shook her head to banish it.

Two miles past the village they came to a break in the hedgerows, where a lane led to a red brick manor house.

The driver paused. "This be it, ma'am?" he called down.

"Yes, indeed," she replied through the open window. Anne closed her eyes and gathered her strength. She reminded herself that she must remember to be calm, and to remain in control. She would show her father that she was no longer a willful child, but rather a grown woman, someone to be reckoned with.

Ian squirmed on the seat as she smoothed back his unruly red hair and tugged his collar into shape. It was important that he make a good first impression. Satisfied that he looked as well as could be expected, she straightened her bonnet, then drew on her gloves.

"Mama, is it Chrismastide in England?"

"No, it is summer, the same as back home."

"Then why is there a wreath on the door?" Ian asked.

Anne's heart caught in her throat. She looked out the window, but the carriage was turning into the circle before the house. As the house came into view, she saw that the windows were closed and shuttered, despite the early summer heat. On the main doors were matching wreaths, trimmed with black ribbons.

Death had visited here. She clung to the faint hope that the mourning was for someone other than the master of the house.

The carriage drew to a halt. A servant approached from the stables and opened the carriage door.

"Something sad has happened here," Anne explained. "Be a good lad and stay in the carriage while I speak with . . . with the staff."

She descended from the carriage and practically ran up the steps, although she knew it was too late for haste. As she reached the top of the stairs, the main door opened before her.

Boswell, the longtime ruler of the servants' hall, stood barring the way within. "We are not receiving visitors," he announced, dismissing her with a mere glance.

"I am not a visitor," Anne said tersely.

The butler gave her a closer look and then recognition dawned. "Miss Anne! I didn't recognize you."

"My father?"

"He went to his reward a fortnight ago. He had

been ill for quite some time now." Boswell had always disapproved of her, and now his voice held a note of reproach, as if her father's passing was somehow her fault.

"I did not know."

Boswell gave her a look of disdain. Then he looked past her, and his eyes widened in apparent shock. "Lord have mercy," he exclaimed.

A small hand crept into hers as Ian came to stand at her side. "Ian, this is Mr. Boswell," she said. "He is the butler, the chief of the servants."

Boswell's mouth opened and closed, but no words came out. She knew exactly what he was seeing. With his flaming red hair and green eyes, Ian bore an uncanny resemblance to herself at his age. "And, Mr. Boswell, this is Master Ian."

"Heaven help us all," the butler replied.

Indeed.

Two

His mother was waiting for him in the breakfast room. For a moment, George Pennington, sixth and possibly last Viscount Frederick, thought of creeping back to his room. But with a sigh he realized that there was no point in postponing the inevitable confrontation. It was best to let his mother have her say now, rather than have her spend all day working herself into a fury.

He squared his shoulders, and advanced into the breakfast room.

"Good morning, Mother. You are up early this morning."

"Dear George," his mother said.

He repressed a wince. He hated that name. Friends called him by his title Frederick or by the nickname Freddie he had acquired, having inherited his title as a small boy. But his mother refused to address him as Freddie, saying that it was a common name.

He approached her chair, and she presented her cheek for him to kiss.

"Naturally I arose at once, after my maid told me that my only son had arrived during the night. I wasn't expecting you and Priscilla for weeks. Is something amiss?"

"There is no cause for alarm," Lord Frederick replied, taking his customary seat at the opposite end of the table from his mother. Pouring himself a cup of coffee he continued, "Prissy left London on a tour of the lakes with Elizabeth and David, as we had planned."

Prissy, the youngest of his five sisters, was also the most unruly, and at eighteen was more than a handful to manage. His mother, who by rights should have been responsible for overseeing Priscilla's come-out, had developed an aversion to London society that coincided with her youngest daughter's coming of age. After a season of watching over Priscilla, it had been with a great deal of relief that Freddie had turned her over to the care of his sister and her new husband.

"Yes, I recall. But were you not planning to attend Lord and Lady Glendale's house party?"

"There are matters here which require my attention, so we agreed to postpone my visit," Freddie said. Although Lord Glendale had urged him to change his mind, Freddie had held firm. He did not begrudge Glendale and Jane their happiness, but he could not bear to see them. Not now, when it felt as if he would never find such happiness for himself.

"Then you *did* get my letter," his mother replied. "I must admit, I had not thought you would be so prompt."

"Letter? Oh, yes, your letter." A letter had arrived just before he'd departed from London. He had not bothered to open it, certain that it contained no more than his mother's usual none-so-subtle hints that it was time he found a wife and began breeding heirs. The letter was probably in his bags somewhere. He would have to find it later.

"Well, now that you are here, you can attend to this matter," his mother said, giving him a rare smile of approval. "I can't imagine what made her think she would be welcome in New Biddeford."

"Indeed." What the devil was his mother talking about?

"I always knew Anne Webster had a wild streak, but I never imagined she would disgrace herself in such a fashion. Showing her face in New Biddeford, still unmarried and not in the least penitent over her situation."

Anne was here? He hadn't seen her for years, and yet he'd thought of her just the other day. Now he wished he had read his mother's letter.

"Even at her age, being unmarried is hardly a crime," Lord Frederick countered. But it was surprising. Nearly seven years ago Anne had left England to visit her sister in Canada. When she didn't return, he'd assumed that she had found a husband and begun a new life.

Lady Frederick set down her knife and fork with a decisiveness that made her china plate ring. Motioning for the footman to leave, she fixed her only son with her best glare, making him feel like a small boy caught in mischief.

"I can not believe that you are defending her. What would you think if it had been your own sister who had returned home with a natural child?"

He swallowed his coffee in such haste that he nearly choked. "A child?"

"Yes, a baseborn brat. And they say he looks just like her."

Anne had come home. Unmarried, but with a child. It was too much to comprehend. His brain refused to wrap itself around the idea. Anne had been willful and impulsive, yes. But he would never have imagined her capable of such an enormous indiscretion. He did not believe it now. It must be a mistake.

"And what does Anne have to say for herself?"

Lady Frederick drew herself up stiffly. "Surely you don't expect that I would lower myself to speak with that trollop? I have not seen her myself, but when I do, I will refuse to acknowledge her."

Freddie fixed his mother with a firm stare. "You will do nothing of the sort. I will not have Anne condemned simply on the strength of malicious gossip. I am certain there must be a reasonable explanation. I will call on her myself, and will have this matter straightened away in no time."

"And when you find the gossip is true? You will have to do your duty and see that she leaves New Biddeford," his mother said.

"I am sure that will not be necessary." It would not. It could not.

Lady Frederick gave a delicate sniff, then turned her attention back to her breakfast. Clearly she considered the matter settled. This was not like her. His mother was perfectly capable of haranguing him for hours, until he agreed to do what she asked. Her easy acceptance of his dismissal of the subject worried him. It meant she was certain of her ground and that no persuasion would be necessary.

He found he had no appetite for breakfast. Freddie excused himself, and went to his study. The correspondence he had brought from London was neatly arranged on his desk. Flipping through the letters, he found an envelope addressed in his mother's hand at the bottom of the pile.

Holding the envelope in one hand, he walked around the desk and sat in the chair. He stared for a moment at the envelope, as if he could somehow divine the contents. Then, with a sigh, he tore it open and began to read.

The Dowager Lady Frederick had found four sheets of paper barely sufficient to describe her moral outrage and distress. She had urged Freddie to come home at once, lest the village slide into an irreversible moral decline. She reminded him of his duty, not once but seven times, and then finished by warning of the dangers to Priscilla's reputation should Anne Webster be allowed to remain.

Lady Frederick did not describe how Anne's presence could possibly affect Priscilla, who was presently one hundred miles away in London. Nor did she elaborate on the circumstances of Anne's return. From reading the letter, he knew no more than he had before. Only two facts seemed clear. Anne had come home at long last and had brought with her a child.

Beyond that. he would reserve his judgment. His mother had never liked Anne. Anne had been an unruly child, who preferred playing crusaders and infidels with Freddie to the more genteel games of his sisters. Whenever Freddie had failed to live up to her standards, Lady Frederick had been quick to blame his failures on Anne's influence.

No doubt this was all a simple misunderstanding.

He had every faith that there was a perfectly reasonable explanation of why Miss Anne Webster should have charge of a child. A few words from Anne would suffice to clear up the matter, and they would laugh together over the foolish gossip.

He glanced at his watch. Nine o'clock. It was too early to call on Anne. Once that would not have stopped him, but they had been mere children. Now he was a gentleman, and there were civilities to be maintained. He had waited seven years to see her. Another few hours could hardly matter. He would wait upon her after lunch, as was civilized.

He heard the village bells strike the hour of ten as he turned his horse into the lane that led to the Websters' estate. So much for his vow to wait patiently, as a gentleman would. Freddie tried, but could not remember the last time that he had visited here. Could it really have been seven years? It seemed impossible. Mr. Webster had been a member of the gentry and the most prominent landowner in the area, save for Lord Frederick. Yet Mr. Webster had been little given to entertainments, and after the death of his wife, he had become a recluse. Out of courtesy Lady Frederick had sent him an invitation to every party held at Beechwood Park, but he had seldom deigned to accept.

Yet the manor house looked much the same as it always had, and the stables were still off to the left. Freddie rode his horse to the stables, noting that the turnout paddock looked unused and most of the stalls were empty. He'd heard that Webster had sold off most of his horses in the years before his death, but it was still disconcerting to see the rows of empty stalls that had once housed some of the finest hunters in the county.

As Freddie dismounted a groom came out to take his horse. A smile creased the groom's weather-beaten face as he recognized the visitor. "Lord Frederick," he said. "Miss Anne will be that glad to see you."

"Thank you, Samson," Freddie said, handing the reins over. "Is she receiving callers?"

"Some yes, some no. But she'll see you for sure," the groom replied.

"There've been a great many changes since I was last here," Freddie said, referring to the empty stables.

The smile left Samson's face. "It's not my place to say," he said stiffly.

Freddie wondered how he could possibly have offended the man. He felt as if he should apologize, if only he knew what for. But he could hardly demand an explanation.

Just then he heard the sound of running feet on the gravel. "Mr. Sammy!" a voice called, and then the figure of a small boy came into sight.

The boy raced up to the groom. "I finished my lessons, and Mama said I could come help you with the horses."

Freddie swallowed hard. The boy looked to be about five or six years of age. And with his bright red hair and copper freckles, he was the image of Anne at that age.

This was no simple misunderstanding. This was a disaster.

Samson's eyes caught and held his, and in his gaze Freddie saw the confirmation of his own worst fears.

"Now where are your manners, Master Ian?" Samson asked. "Did you not see this gentleman?"

The boy turned toward Freddie. "I am sorry, sir," he said.

Freddie could see Samson was watching to see what he would do next. A part of him grew angry. Did the groom think so little of him as to imagine that he would scorn the boy simply because of his birth?

"I am Viscount Frederick," he said, extending his hand. "A friend of your mother's."

Young Ian shook Freddie's hand with as much vigor as he could muster. "I am pleased to make your acquaintance Mr. Frederick."

"Lord Frederick," Samson corrected him. "The gentleman is a viscount."

The boy stared at him as if he had grown another head. "A real lord? With castles and knights and all?"

"Not quite like that."

Ian bore this disappointment philosophically. "I should have guessed. A real knight would have worn his armor."

Freddie quelled the urge to defend his family's honor by pointing out that the first Lord Frederick had indeed been a knight, with a castle of sorts. Not much of a castle, but the ruins were still there, as proof of his family's ancient heritage.

But he had not come here to explain English history to Master Ian. He could save that for another day. For now, having seen the boy, it was even more urgent that he see Anne.

"It was a pleasure to make your acquaintance, Master Ian," Freddie said. It was also the shock of his life, but there was no reason to let the boy know that. "And now I will leave you to Samson while I go see your mother."

Three

A footman showed him into the formal drawing room. "Miss Webster will be with you presently," he said. Still unsettled by the sight of young Ian, Freddie willed himself to be calm. He was burning with curiosity, but he vowed that he would not be the first to raise the subject of her supposed son. He would respect her privacy and let Anne tell him what she would.

Then he heard her voice. "Kindly inform Mrs. Perry that I have finished the inventory of the linens, and I will join her as soon as I may."

"Yes, miss," a voice replied.

Then Anne came into sight.

At first she looked a stranger, her auburn hair tightly pulled back and a white apron covering her dark gray gown. He looked in vain for some trace of the old Anne, whose curls would never stay tamed and whose gowns, more often than not, had a flounce ripped from her carefree adventures.

And then her eyes caught his, and he knew at once that this was indeed Anne.

Her gaze was wary. "Lord Frederick, how kind of you to call. As you can see, I was not expecting visitors," she said, gesturing with one hand to indicate her apron and gloveless state.

Lord Frederick, indeed. What did she mean by this sudden formality? In the past she had only called him by his title when she was angry with him.

He crossed the space that divided them and took her hands in his. "Anne, it is good to see you. I came as soon as I learned you were here."

She did not pull her hands away, but neither did a smile lighten her face. "You mean to say that your mother sent you. I am certain the Dowager Lady Frederick had much to say on the subject of my arrival."

He gave her hands a gentle squeeze. "I am fortunate my mother mentioned your presence," he said diplomatically. "Why did you not write me and tell me that you had returned?"

Some of the wariness left her eyes. She gently disentangled her hands from his. "Please sit down," she said. "Let me ring for refreshments."

She rang the bell, then seated herself in a wingback chair. Freddie chose a seat on the sofa opposite her. Within moments a footman appeared.

"Lemonade? Or do you prefer something stronger these days?"

"Lemonade will be fine," he assured her.

"Then have Cook send lemonade, and some of the biscuits she made this morning," Anne instructed.

It was all so civil. So genteel and well mannered. Yet at the same time, it was all wrong. He and Anne had never stood on ceremony in their lives, yet now she was treating him as a mere acquaintance.

"So, why did you not write of your arrival?" Freddie asked. Unspoken was the thought, why had he not heard from her before? Once they had been as close as two friends could be. And then seven years had passed. Seven long years, and in all that time not a single letter. Not one. Not even a message given to her father to relay to him. Anything could have happened to her over there, and he would never have known.

His mind pulled up short. Something had, indeed, happened, as witnessed by the presence of young Ian.

"I did not have your direction. And even if I had, I am not certain it would have been proper for me to write. Your wife might not have understood."

"There is no Lady Frederick," he said.

Anne appeared surprised. "Still a bachelor? I find it hard to believe that after all these years on the town, no lady has captured your heart."

"Still a bachelor, to my mother's eternal despair, I might add."

Anne chuckled at his rueful expression. "Poor Freddie. I imagine she exhorts you constantly to do your duty and secure the line."

"Not more than once a fortnight," he said. "And you?"

As soon as the words were out of his mouth, he regretted them.

"Still Miss Webster, as you have no doubt heard." Her tone was positively frosty.

He fought for something to say, but nothing came to mind that did not seem patronizing or accusatory. He was rescued by the arrival of the footman, bearing a tray of biscuits and a pitcher of lemonade.

Anne poured out two glasses and handed one to him. He took a sip of lemonade, then bit into the biscuit. It was soft and chewy, and the taste of molasses brought back memories of his childhood. How many times had he and Anne sat in the kitchen of this very house while Cook plied them with biscuits and lemonade?

He sighed with pure happiness. "Ah, I had forgotten how much I missed this. And you, of course."

"Dear Freddie. I always knew Cook came first in your affections and I a distant second," Anne teased. The awkwardness of a moment before was forgotten.

"True. But could we combine your beauty with Cook's talent for baking, then we would have my ideal woman."

"No wonder you have found no wife. You should cease courting the ladies of the *ton*, and seek out baker's assistants instead."

Freddie stroked his chin. "The idea has merit," he said in mock solemnity. "I shall give it serious consideration."

The moment of levity passed, and the silence stretched between them. Where once the silence would have been companionable, now it was uncomfortable, reminding him of how little he knew of how she had spent the past years. A half-dozen topics came to mind, and were as quickly discarded. Strange that he, veteran of hundreds of drawing rooms, should find himself with nothing to say. Yet

Anne would have no interest in the gossip of London, though no other topic came to mind that did not seem either trite or damning.

And Anne showed no sign of being willing to speak first.

"I was sorry to hear of your father's passing. Did you have a chance to see him before the end?" he asked, broaching the stated purpose of his call.

She shook her head. "He died a fortnight before my arrival."

It was a cruel trick of fate that she had journeyed so far only to find she had come too late. "I am sorry for that as well. It must have been a dreadful disappointment to you."

She nodded gravely. "I thank you for your kind sentiments."

Her face was calm and gave no hint of whether or not she was grieving for her father's passing. Anne's father had been a hard man. A difficult man to love or even like. Freddie would not blame her if she found it difficult to mourn him, and yet, after all, he had been her father and only living parent.

Freddie was frustrated by his inability to read Anne. Once she had worn her emotions on her face so all could tell how she felt. But in the years that she had been away, she had learned to hide her feelings. Was this simply a consequence of maturity? Or had some painful lesson forced her to learn to dissemble?

"Will you be making your home here?"

Anne's chin came up, and there was a flash of her old fire in her green eyes.

"You may tell your mother not to fret. I will stay only long enough to wind up my father's affairs, and then I will return to my home."

He sensed that she was braced for condemnation, and he was angry that she thought so little of him.

"I am sorry to hear that. I had hoped you had returned to stay," Freddie said. "But I understand that you must have ties in Canada as well now."

He would miss her if she left, yet he did not blame her for not wanting to remain. He suspected more than a few self-righteous souls had gone out of their way to make sure Anne knew how little they welcomed her presence. And he knew nothing of her life in Canada. Perhaps there was someone there she held in affection.

"You must be the only person in New Biddeford who does not wish me gone posthaste."

He could hear the bitterness in her voice. He wanted to cheer her up. To wipe away the sadness and wariness that seemed so much a part of this new Anne. He wanted to hold her, to assure her that he would make everything better. But this was not a mere scraped knee or a broken doll. To all evidence, Anne had committed the most grievous sin that a young woman could commit. As a gentleman, it should be beneath him to acknowledge the sin, let alone the sinner. Unless she asked for his help, there was very little he could do. The chains of custom and propriety had never before weighed as heavily as they did now.

He did the only thing he could.

"Remember you can count on my friendship," he said. "While you are here, let us not be strangers. Do not hesitate to call on me, should you need anything. Anything at all."

"I will remember."

And with that promise, he had to be content.

A polite cough indicated the presence of a maid, hovering in the doorway. "Begging your pardon, Miss Anne, but Mrs. Perry needs to speak with you."

"I must go," Anne said, rising from her chair.

"And I as well." Freddie rose from his seat and followed Anne to the door. "I hope I may call on you again."

"I would like that very much."

Freddie took his hat and gloves from the table in the entranceway. "Please give my respects to Master Ian, and tell him how much I enjoyed making his acquaintance."

The look on her face was priceless. He could tell she was shocked by his casual mention of Ian, when they had spent the last half-hour carefully dancing around any mention of the boy or the scandalous rumors attached to his presence. Yet he wanted Anne to know that he had met Ian and that he was making no judgments.

She had forgotten his kindness. She had remembered his appearance, his smile and even his fondness for lemonade and Cook's freshly baked biscuits. But she had forgotten the kindness that was such an essential part of Freddie's nature.

Or was it that she had not dared hope he would show her his kindness? Throughout their visit she had been unable to relax, certain that at any moment he would reveal the true purpose of his visit. A polite, yet firm request that she remove her scandalous presence from the neighborhood. Or, worse yet, that he would ask her questions she dare not answer.

Yet he had said nothing, giving every appearance that he was genuinely glad to see her and to renew their friendship. It might have been any social call, the undercurrent of awkwardness explainable by the long years they had been apart.

So she had reasoned, and she had allowed herself the selfish pleasure of enjoying the visit for its own sake. Freddie was the first caller who had not greeted her with scorn. She would let herself enjoy the moment, knowing that all too soon his attitude would change.

His promise of friendship, despite anything, had reminded her that he had heard the gossip. And then he had shocked her with the news that he had already encountered Ian. Surely having seen Ian, Freddie would have leapt to the same conclusions that everyone else had. Even those servants who had been loyal to her in the old days had taken one look at Ian and concluded that this was her child.

To be fair, it was not strictly the servants' fault. From what she could gather, in his last days her father had raged on about his ungrateful daughter and the bastard son she had borne. Her and Ian's arrival had seemed proof of his ravings. And such gossip was too good to be kept to themselves. Within hours of Anne's arrival, the news had spread throughout the neighborhood. By now, the gossip would have reached London. Not that anyone there would care about the doings of Miss Anne Webster, spinster daughter of obscure country gentry.

She could have put a halt to the gossip by showing her marriage lines. But she could not, for there were none. And so, condemned by her father in his death as she had been during his lifetime, Anne planned to leave New Biddeford as soon as possible.

Consequently, she had gritted her teeth and endured the condolence call from the vicar's wife. Mrs. Poundstone, however, had proven more interested in lecturing Anne on the state of her soul than on consoling her in her supposed grief.

Mrs. Poundstone had been a model of propriety when compared to the Misses Hamiltons. Middle-aged spinsters, the two ladies had welcomed Anne back to the neighborhood with insincere warmth, then had proceeded to ask the most impertinent questions regarding Ian's exact age and the circumstances of his birth. This Anne had refused to endure, and she had unceremoniously ejected the women from the house.

It was no wonder then that she had expected Freddie to treat her coldly. Surely his mother had seen fit to apprise him of the gossip that was circulating concerning Anne and her supposed son. Yet in spite of what he had heard, and what he had seen with his own eyes, if Freddie had drawn any conclusions he had kept them to himself. He had gone out of his way to make her feel welcome and to assure her of his continued friendship.

In her mind, such kindness and loyalty were the

mark of a true gentleman. Although she doubted that the Dowager Lady Frederick would agree. And if there was anyone with whom she felt inclined to share her burden, it would have been her old friend. But the secret of Ian's birth was not hers alone to keep, and so she kept silent.

She wondered if Freddie would call again. Her heart hoped so, and yet she knew it was foolish of her. She would be gone in a few weeks, this time never to return. But while she was here, it was good to know she had at least one true friend.

Four

Freddie's visit stood out as the one bright spot in a week of misery. Anne had half-expected to see him again, and had scolded herself for being disappointed that he made no further effort to seek her out. No doubt his mother, the dowager Lady Frederick, had used her influence to make her son think better of encouraging the connection.

The days passed slowly. By her own choice she would have left as soon as she learned of her father's death, but her time was not her own. Her father's solicitor had left a letter requesting that she notify him upon her arrival so that he could wait upon her. She had written to him at once, but she had waited nearly two weeks before Mr. Creighton condescended to let her know that he would be calling on her the next day.

For the hundredth time, she wondered why the solicitor wished to see her. Was it simply to inform her that she had no legal right to stay at the residence? Her father had disowned her years before, so there was no hope of an inheritance. The most she could hope for was that her father had relented sufficiently to allow her the portrait of her mother or some other items of sentimental value. Knowing her father's character, it was more likely that he had dictated one final diatribe and now expected his solicitor to deliver the message for him.

Still, there was no use fretting. She owed her father this one final duty, and then she and Ian would leave. She had already booked their passage on a ship that would sail for Lower Canada within the fortnight.

Looking out the window of the drawing room, Anne saw a hired carriage coming up the drive. A glance at the clock confirmed that it lacked but a few minutes until noon, the hour Mr. Creighton had appointed for his call.

Swiftly she moved to a chair and picked up the book of poetry she had discarded earlier. She did not want Mr. Creighton to see how nervous she was.

The door opened, without so much as a knock, and a housemaid announced, "Mr. Creighton to see you, miss." There was a studied insolence in the maid's tone. Although a few of the servants were loyal to her, most had followed the lead of the butler, Mr. Boswell. He would never have permitted her to stay on that first day, had the solicitor not left instructions that he expected to call on her at her father's house. As it was, the servants, unsure if she was their new mistress or merely an interloper, treated her with scant courtesy or respect.

The gentleman who entered the room was not the formidable friend of her father, but rather a much younger man.

"Adam Creighton at your service, Miss Webster," he said with a bow.

She guessed at once that this was Mr. Creighton,

the younger, who must have joined his father's firm. There was a distinct family resemblance in his features and in the unfortunate way that his ears stood out from his head.

"Mr. Creighton, I am pleased to make your acquaintance," Anne said, laying down the book she had just picked up. "Pray be seated."

The solicitor glanced around, then chose a seat on the sofa, placing his satchel on the table before him. Uncertain of his purpose, she did not offer refreshments, not wishing to prolong his visit any longer than necessary. It was discourteous, but he did not seem to notice the slight.

Mr. Creighton reached into his pocket and withdrew a pair of spectacles which he then perched on the bridge of his nose. The spectacles made him look even younger than before, as if he were a boy playing at his father's profession. Then he opened the satchel and withdrew a sheaf of papers tied with a crimson ribbon.

"My condolences to you on your loss. It must have come as a great shock," he said diffidently.

"You are too kind," she said, then could not resist adding, "But I had expected you somewhat earlier."

"I regret having made you wait, but there was another client of mine who required my services most urgently. It seemed there was no harm in the delay."

"And your father did not wish to perform the errand himself."

"Er . . ." Mr. Creighton's face flushed with embarrassment. With one hand he tugged a neckcloth that had suddenly grown too tight. "Well, you see, that is, upon all due consideration, and er, considering the, ahem, the circumstances, as it were . . ."

His eyes darted around the room as if he were seeking escape.

Anne felt a twinge of sympathy for the young man. Whatever message her father had left, it must be worse than she had feared.

"Mr. Creighton, you can be certain that whatever my father had to say, it is nothing that he has not written or said to me before. Simply give me his message, and then we will be done with it."

Mr. Creighton took a deep breath, as if to calm himself. Then he untied the scarlet ribbon and rifled through the sheaf till he found the piece of paper he was looking for.

"As you know, your late father was a man of considerable property. Not wealthy, mind you, but I venture to say that he had more than sufficient means to live comfortably, as befitted a gentleman."

Comfortably. Anne suppressed a bitter laugh. She and Ian had subsisted all these years on a tiny fraction of what her father's properties brought in during a year.

The solicitor continued. "As your father's estate was not entailed, its disposition was left to his discretion. With no male heirs, originally the property was to be divided between you and your sister. Then, in his final years, your father amended the will. First, when your mother passed on, and later, upon the death of your sister. This last year he made one final alteration."

Would he never come to the point? "You do not need to tell me any more. I know that my father had written me out of his will. It was the last I heard from him, until he sent for me this spring."

"Yes. Indeed. Well, as you say, there was no pro-

vision made for you," he said, appearing grateful
that she was not the type to make an unpleasant
scene. "But as guardian, you will, of course, have
access to the funds from the estate until the boy
reaches his majority. To enable you to pay for his
upkeep and schooling and the like."

Guardian? Surely she had misheard. "I am afraid
I do not understand."

"Of course, you are not the sole guardian. I am
named as well, as a trustee. But your father's will
made it quite clear that the principal responsibility
rests with you." Here the solicitor paused, frowning.
"I am not certain that it is wise to put such responsibility into the hands of a woman, but it was what
your father wanted."

An idea occurred that was at once preposterous,
and yet at the same time . . . "I still do not understand. I am to be a guardian, for whom?"

"For the child, of course." The lawyer adjusted
his spectacles and began to read from the document
he held. "I leave my estate to the child known as
Ian Webster, who resides in the care of my daughter
Anne, and whom I now acknowledge as my grandson."

For a moment it seemed as if her heart would
stop. Never had she expected this. "Ian? Ian is to
inherit all this?" she asked with a wave of her hand
meant to encompass the house and estate.

"Yes. I thought you understood that." Mr.
Creighton peered over the document at her. "The
estate is his. To be held in trust until he reaches
his majority."

She could not understand why her father had

done such a thing. "And what of Ian's parentage? Did he say anything more?" She had to know.

Mr. Creighton flushed. Even as she awaited his answer, a part of her mind observed that his fair skin must be a severe trial in his chosen profession.

"There is nothing more written, save what you have already heard." His voice stressed the word written.

"Nothing more written. But what else did he say?" Surely he would not acknowledge Ian without also acknowledging Anne's innocence.

"I regret that I can not break any confidences that he may have shared with me. What is important is that he recognized the boy as his grandson and made more than generous provision for him, considering the, er, the irregularities of his birth."

She swallowed against the lump that rose in her throat. Even to the last, her father had refused to forgive her. Somehow, he had blamed her for what had happened. True, Ian would never want for anything again, but she bitterly resented that her father had not seen fit to include her in his belated attempts to set things right.

Would it have made any difference if she had arrived before his death? Or would he have continued to condemn her, reserving his care for Ian, the one true innocent in all that had happened?

She gradually became aware that Mr. Creighton was still droning on.

"Now, there are several decisions that need to be made," he said. "You may draw upon the accounts to pay the expenses of the household, the servants' wages and such, but you will need to decide if you are to reside here or if you wish to rent the estate.

Of course, you could sell the estate, but there is no need for such a hasty decision. Prudence and caution will serve you well—"

"Enough," Anne said sharply. She felt torn between hysterical laughter and tears of outrage. Her father had written a will that provided for her and Ian to live comfortably all their lives, yet at the same time had ensured she would never be able to overcome her tarnished reputation. It was an act of unspeakable cruelty. For her pride's sake, she wished she could refuse the inheritance, but she could not sacrifice Ian's future for the sake of her wounded feelings.

"I appreciate your concern, but you must realize this news comes as quite a surprise. I need time to ponder my choices. Perhaps you would be so kind as to return another day, when we can discuss these affairs at leisure." So saying, Anne rose, and out of courtesy Mr. Creighton rose as well.

"I have a very busy schedule," he objected. "But if you insist—"

"I do." Far better that she send Mr. Creighton away. In her current mood, she did not trust herself to discuss her father or his affairs and keep a civil tongue in her head. She needed time alone, to come to terms with what her father had done.

At least one of the servants must have been listening at the door during her conversation with Mr. Creighton. Or perhaps not one, but all of them. Anne was hard put to blame them for their curiosity. After all, the contents of her father's will would determine their fate as well. If the manor was to be closed up or sold off, they would lose their positions. And in these hard times, positions were difficult to come by.

However they knew, the change in their attitude toward her was both swift and profound. That day, when Mr. Creighton went to leave, it was a footman and not a mere maid who brought the solicitor his hat and gloves. And in the days that had passed, Anne's tea arrived while it was still hot, housemaids answered her summons rather than requiring Anne to seek them out and Cook outdid herself preparing Anne's favorite meals. Anne might be branded a sinner, but as long as she continued to pay their wages, the servants seemed prepared to forgive any past indiscretions. And through their efforts, they seemed determined to convince her to stay.

Only the butler, Mr. Boswell, had persisted in his scorn for her. His service was perfectly correct, but she fancied she could see the contempt for her that hid behind his eyes. Not to mention his loathsome habit of referring to her as "Miss Anne" at every opportunity, stressing the title of Miss as a constant reminder of the shame of her unwedded state. Anne determined that she would pension him off at the earliest opportunity.

She wondered if the newfound tolerance extended past the manor gates. Unlike the servants, the villagers had no reason to be grateful to her. And she had no doubt that her father's will and its implications were being hotly debated in the drawing rooms and taprooms of New Biddeford. She wondered what they were saying about her. Was it too much to hope that this would be a nine days' wonder, and some new scandal would arise to distract them all?

Well, she would know soon enough. Though she had put off this trip for days, she could delay no longer. There had been only so much that she could bring from Canada, and with the summer approaching the wool gowns she had brought were rapidly becoming unbearable.

She had thought to make over some of her old garments, but it was not possible. Anne had been shocked to discover that her father had disposed of every trace of her and Sarah's presence. Not a single dress or pair of shoes remained from the days before she had left for Canada. Even their dolls were gone from the nursery, their books from the schoolroom. It was as if she and Sarah had never existed, and it gave her the oddest sense of being a stranger in the home of her childhood.

Fortunately there was a dressmaker in New Biddeford, as well as a linen shop where she could purchase fabric to make Ian new shirts. Lately it seemed that he outgrew his clothes nearly as fast as she could make them.

Anne made a list of what she needed, then sought out Ian to let him know that she was leaving.

"May I come too?" he asked.

"No, dear," Anne said. "But I won't be long. And when I return we will have our tea on the lawn. Cook has promised to make ginger biscuits and lemon snaps."

Though yesterday Ian had begged for such a treat, today this was not enough to distract him. "But, Mama, we have been here ever so long. And you never have time for me anymore."

He looked so forlorn one would think she had
confined him to his room, rather than letting him
run free over the manor grounds. Grounds which
could easily hold the entire village where they lived
back in Canada.

"Please, Mama? I'll be ever so good. I promise."

Anne hesitated, afraid. She did not know what she
feared, yet deep inside her she felt reluctant to expose Ian to the world outside the gates. She would
not rest easy until they had returned to Canada and
could sink back into quiet anonymity. Still, what
harm could there be? They might not be friendly,
but it was unlikely the shopkeepers would be rude
to her. And surely no one would say anything to a
child.

"Very well. Go wash your hands and face, and
fetch your cap."

An hour later, she was glad that she had agreed
to Ian's company. It cheered her to see how much
he enjoyed the outing. He was a constant bundle of
energy, marveling over the stone buildings, the
placid sheep grazing on the green, even the
millpond and its ducks. Everything that she took for
granted, he found marvelous and exciting, because
it was so different from the seaside village that had
been his world before now.

He was even patient, in his own way, as she called
on the village dressmaker and ordered two gowns
made up. They were both walking dresses, one of a
plain dark gray fabric and the other of a dark brown
patterned in black. It had taken much persuasion to
convince the dressmaker to fashion the two garments, the dressmaker insisting that only black would
do. But Anne had refused to be a hypocrite. She

would not don full mourning for a parent who had treated her so cruelly. At last she and the dressmaker had agreed on these sober fabrics as a compromise. Anne and Ian left, Anne having been assured that the gowns would be ready within two days.

Outside the shop, Ian asked, "Can we go home now?"

As the afternoon had worn on, he'd finally seemed to reach the limits of his energy. His eyes were tired, and he walked sedately by her side instead of skipping ahead.

"Just one more shop, I promise. Then we will go home and have our tea."

The lending library was on the way back to the top of the village where she had left the pony cart. Along with the rest of their possessions, Anne had left her books behind in Canada. Now, with their stay prolonged, she would welcome the diversion of a novel. And Ian had been idle for much too long. It was time to resume his lessons; for that she would need a primer.

Ian's eyes brightened as she paused at the door to the lending library. Books were a rare and precious treat, and next to his riding lessons, he loved nothing better than to sit in Anne's lap as she read to him.

"Now be careful not to touch anything. But if you are very good you may choose a picture book for your own."

Ian promised, and into the library they went.

It had been over a week since he had seen Anne. Every day he promised himself that today would be the day he called on her. Yet each day came and went, and the promise went unfulfilled.

It was partly his mother's fault. The Dowager Lady Frederick had not been pleased when he'd returned from his first visit to Anne and revealed that he had not ordered her to leave the neighborhood. Finally, to secure some peace, he had promised his mother he would take the matter under consideration.

When Lady Frederick asked him point-blank what his feelings were toward Anne, he had told her honestly that he did not know. Seeing her again had felt good, as if a part of his past had returned to him. And yet there was the child, who bore witness that Anne was not the innocent she seemed.

A part of him wanted to go to her, to demand the name of the man who had seduced her and then had left her to bear her shame alone. He would see that the cad paid for his crimes.

Yet another part of him held back, half-afraid that Anne did not want to be avenged. He could not imagine her giving herself to any man whom she did not love. And the coward in him did not want to confront Anne, only to hear how she had loved another.

And so he had stayed away, trying to think his way through this dilemma. Sensing his wavering feelings toward Anne, his mother, with the complicity of their longtime steward, invented dozens of obligations and errands that Freddie must see to personally.

Even now he was on his way to New Biddeford, running another errand for his mother. He was not quite sure how it had happened. One moment his mother was complaining about how she had nothing to divert her, and the next he had agreed to fetch her a selection of the latest novels. Eager to escape his mother's constant harping, if only for a few hours, Freddie did not bother to ask why his mother, who still exercised her own mare every day regardless of the weather, was suddenly unable to make the journey herself.

As he entered the lending library, he knew there must be something out of the ordinary occurring. For once his entrance went unremarked, as the patrons had their attention focused on a commotion at the back of the room. But there were too many people in the way for him to see what was going on.

"We don't want your patronage. Get out, and if you know what is good for you, you will never return."

Freddie recognized the speaker as Tom Sweet, who was chief clerk. He could not hear the low-voiced reply, but some instinct warned him there was trouble, and he began threading his way among the bookcases and tables, toward the back of the room. There he found a dozen or so onlookers, standing in a semicircle before the clerk's counter.

"Does not the Bible say 'Judge not and ye shall not be judged'?"

He could not see her, but he would recognize Anne's voice anywhere.

"Pardon me," Freddie said, tapping on the shoulder of Mr. Steerwell.

"Of course, my lord," Steerwell said, turning sideways so Freddie could squeeze by his bulk. "Reckon you'll want to see this. That trollop Anne Webster is getting her comeuppance."

Freddie glared at Steerwell, but he had more important matters to attend to.

Encouraged by murmurs from the audience, Tom Sweet continued his harangue. "Your presence in New Biddeford is a disgrace. Any decent woman would know better than to parade her bas—"

"Enough." It was not quite a shout.

Tom Sweet's jaw snapped shut as he saw who had spoken.

Anne turned to him. Her cheeks were flushed and her eyes sparked with anger. "I can take care of myself," she insisted.

"Of course you can," he lied.

Next to her, he could see the boy Ian, who seemed bewildered by the confrontation.

"And good day to you, Master Ian."

Anne nudged him, and the boy executed a creditable bow. "Good afternoon, Lord Frederick," he said.

Freddie turned his attention back to the impertinent clerk. As a boy, Tom Sweet had been a bully, always picking on those weaker than himself. It seemed that little had changed.

Freddie fixed the clerk with his gaze, letting him feel the full weight of his displeasure. "It seems a mistake has been made. I believe you owe Miss Webster an apology."

"But, sir—"

"An apology. Now. Or do you truly wish to seek employment elsewhere?" It would take no more than a word from Freddie to see that Tom Sweet lost his job—and all hope of employment elsewhere in the county. It was a power he seldom used, but in this instance it would be a pleasure.

Tom Sweet licked his pale lips. "Of course. My lord, I am sorry if you were offended."

"It is Miss Webster whose pardon you should beg."

Anne drew a breath, but he placed his hand on her arm, forestalling whatever remark she was about to make.

Tom Sweet began again. "Miss Webster, it seems I have been misinformed. I apologize for my hasty remarks, and hope that you will not hold them against me."

It was not graceful, but he knew it was all the man was capable of.

Anne inclined her head. "I accept your apology."

He marveled at her restraint. The old Anne would have given the clerk the verbal tongue-lashing of his life. But now, seemingly conscious of young Ian hanging on her every word, Anne held her tongue.

Freddie stayed at her side as she concluded her business, then escorted her and Ian from the shop.

Once they were on the street, away from curious listeners, Anne turned to him. "You did not have to interfere," she said testily.

"Would you have liked it better if I had stood by and said nothing?"

This surprised a faint smile out of her. "No, I suppose not," she said.

Her smile disappeared as quickly as it had come. He could see the lines of strain on her face, and he wondered just what had been said before he had arrived on the scene? How many others had seen fit to insult her? He could not understand how they could do such a thing to one of their own, a girl they had known all her life.

He felt a stab of guilt as he realized that he himself was little better. After all, he had professed friendship and then had done his best to avoid her.

"Mama, why was that man yelling at you?"

Anne reached down and patted Ian's shoulder. "There is nothing to worry about. It was just a misunderstanding."

Ian nodded, but he still looked miserable, and he was blinking back tears. Freddie suspected that the boy understood more of what had occurred than Anne gave him credit for.

"Is there anything I can do for you? Anything at all?"

Anne shook her head. "No. I thank you, but you have done quite enough for one day."

It was all so unfair. Freddie glanced up and down the street, but no inspiration appeared. He refused to let things end like this, to let Anne walk off without a word. Yet he could hardly invite her back to his estate, not without risking an even uglier confrontation with his mother.

He took her arm and led her toward the top of the village, where Anne had left the pony cart. He knew his time was running out, but nothing occurred to him until he caught sight of his horse Ajax, tied to a hitching post on the green.

Freddie reached down and tapped Ian on the arm. "See that horse over there? The big black one? That's my horse, Ajax."

Ian lifted his drooping head. His eyes widened as he caught sight of Ajax. "He's really yours? He's e-nor-mous. May I pet him?" Without bothering to wait for permission, Ian ran across the green to where the horse was tethered.

"Wait," Anne called, gathering up her skirts and preparing to run after him. "Wait, Ian," she called.

Freddie caught her arm. "There is no need to worry. Ajax is a fraud. I named him after a mighty warrior, but he is the gentlest horse I know. Ian will be perfectly safe," he reassured her.

And indeed they could see it was so, for Ian had already reached the horse, and Ajax had lowered his head so the boy could pat his mane.

Anne slowed to merely a swift walk, but allowed him to guide her around the green rather than muddying their shoes by crossing it.

"Ian looks like he could use a treat. What say I take him up on Ajax and let him ride with me? I promise to return him safe and sound," Freddie said, with a studied attempt at casualness. Even as he issued the invitation, he wondered how much it was prompted by a genuine wish to cheer up a young boy and how much it was due to the knowledge that returning Ian to his mother would give him an excuse to spend more time with Anne?

Anne gave him a look that said she could see right through his scheme. He expected her to refuse, but to his surprise she agreed. "There is no one else I would trust him with," she said. "Just keep the ride a short one. Cook is preparing a special picnic for tea today, and I would hate her preparations to go to waste."

"And I am invited?" Freddie asked boldly.

"Of course. Now, off with you both, before I change my mind."

Five

Freddie lifted Ian up and set him on Ajax's back, just before the saddle.

"Now hold tight to his mane. There's a lad," Freddie said, as he made sure Ian was firmly settled. Then he swung up onto the saddle behind the boy. A more skittish mount might have shown signs of alarm, but the unflappable Ajax merely turned his head to ensure that it was indeed his master on his back.

Anne looked at the two of them doubtfully. "Straight home, and no galloping," she cautioned.

"Yes, Mama," Ian said.

"Don't worry. I'll look after him," Freddie promised. It was only a short ride, not an expedition into the wilds.

He settled his arms around the boy, the reins held firmly in his hands, then started Ajax off at a walk. Even without turning around, he knew that Anne's gaze followed their progress until she could no longer see them.

As they made their way down the High Street, Freddie could see heads turning to watch their progress. This was not unusual. After all, he was the local lord. More than half the villagers made their living working on his estate or supplying those who did. Yet for once there was no one calling his name, nor inquiries after his health. Even Betsy, the tavern maid, sweeping the yard in front of the tavern, forbore to offer him her usual curtsey and cheeky invitation to stop awhile.

He knew their disapproval was not for him, but rather for young Ian. Even after witnessing the ugly confrontation at the lending library, he still found it difficult to believe that they could be so harsh and unforgiving.

Ian made a small sound of protest as Freddie's arm instinctively tightened around him. Freddie forced himself to relax his grip. No matter how tightly he held him, he could not protect the boy from the ill will of the villagers. But he did not relax until they had left the disapproving inhabitants of New Biddeford behind them.

As he turned off the High Street onto the lane that led toward the Websters', he checked on the boy seated before him. Ian had relaxed his death grip on Ajax's mane and was now looking about with interest.

"What do you think of my horse? Do you like him?"

"He's very tall," Ian said noncommittally.

Freddie hesitated, wondering what to say next. His own nieces and nephews were still infants, and he could not remember the last time he had conversed with a young boy.

"You like horses, don't you?" he finally asked.

"Oh, very much. At home we never had a horse, but now Mr. Sammy is teaching me to ride. Sometimes he calls me a proper heathen, but yesterday he said I might make a rider after all."

"That's very high praise. Samson has been teaching children to ride for nearly twenty years. Why, he even taught your mother, and many said she had the best seat for a woman in the county." Whether riding sidesaddle or no, but that was a tale for another day.

Ian twisted around, and looked at Freddie in apparent disbelief. "Mama never rides. And if she was so good, why doesn't she teach me herself?"

Anne had given up riding, once the chief joy of her life? Often in the hunt she had matched him jump for jump, and he would have sworn that nothing would have made her give up riding. Could she really have changed that much?

"Perhaps she is too busy," Freddie said, then wished he could take the words back as he felt Ian's frame sag with unhappiness. "But I think she wanted Sam to teach you so you could learn from the best."

His words did little to comfort the boy.

"Mama is always busy," the boy muttered. "Since we came here, she never has time for me. There is always one of those stiff people around."

"Stiff people?"

"You know. The ones who look at me like I haven't washed my face, even when I know it is clean. Like Mr. Boswell."

"Ah. You mean the servants."

Freddie wondered just how much Ian understood. Did the boy know what it meant to be a bastard? It was too much to expect a child to understand, yet surely the boy knew that something was wrong.

"I hate this place. Mama is never happy since we

came here. I wish we could go home and that everything would be as it was before," Ian said angrily, then banged his heels into the horse's side.

At this signal Ajax sprang forward into a canter. Ian crowed with glee. Freddie's hands tightened on the reins, then loosened. Let the boy have his fun. Freddie felt a keen sympathy with Ian's urge for speed. If only they could run fast enough to outrun their troubles.

"Would you like me to show you how to jump?"

Anne must have been waiting by a window, for she appeared on the stairs before they had reached the top of the drive. A servant held the horse's head as Freddie handed young Ian down and then dismounted himself.

"Mama, Mama!" Ian ran across the gravel drive. "Lord Freddie showed me how to jump. Ajax just ran and ran and then he lifted himself and flew right over the logs. And Lord Freddie said I was a regular trooper and would be a fine hunter one day."

"Oh, he did, did he?" Anne gave Freddie a look that promised retribution. Then she turned her attention to the child. "You can tell me all about it later. Now, in the house with you and wash up, or there will be no tea for you."

Ian dashed indoors, and the two of them were left alone.

"How could you be so thoughtless? He's barely learning to ride and you let him jump? Didn't you stop to think of the harm that could happen? Or how I might feel? I spent the last hour imagining all sorts of dreadful things that might have happened to Ian."

He hadn't realized that Anne would be worried. "I am sorry—"

"Sorry is not good enough. I expected more of you."

He felt as if he were a small boy who had been caught misbehaving. "I apologize," he said, and then spoiled the effect by smiling.

"And wipe that smile off your face. The least you can do is look repentant."

"Forgive me," he said. "It is just that for one moment you sounded so much like my mother I felt it was she and not you who was calling me to task."

Anne sighed and pushed aside a strand of hair that had fallen onto her face. "Now that I have responsibility for a child of my own, I find myself much more in sympathy with Lady Frederick. You must have frightened her half to death with your antics. And now you go teaching Ian your old tricks."

She appeared more resigned than angry. He took that as a good sign. "Truly I did not mean to worry you. I know I promised I would bring him straight here, but Ian seemed low in spirits and I wanted to cheer him up. The home farm was on our way here, so there seemed no harm in a slight delay. It was just a single set of crossed rails, not even two feet high."

Anne raised her eyebrows. "And do you think that will be the end of it? Now he will be after Samson to teach him how to jump on his own pony."

"I hadn't thought of that," he confessed. He had known there was no risk of harm to the boy, as long as they were mounted on Ajax. But he should have realized that Ian was unlikely to be satisfied until he had repeated the experience. As a boy Freddie had been much the same way himself. "If you like, I will try to explain to Ian that he is too young to try jumping on his own."

"No, you can leave that task for me."

Ian chose this moment to reappear, dashing down the stairs and holding his hands out for Anne's inspection.

"Very good," she said, nodding approvingly. She hesitated for a moment, then turned back to Freddie and said, "Will you join us? Cook has prepared a picnic, and I thought to take it down by the stream."

"It would be my pleasure," he said. He led Ajax off to the stables and gave him over to the groom, then met up with Anne and Ian at the kitchen door. Anne held a basket in one hand and carried a blanket in the other. He took the basket in his left hand, then gave the blanket to young Ian. "A gentleman always carries things for his lady," he said.

The boy nodded and clutched the blanket to his chest.

Freddie offered his right arm to Anne. She hesitated a moment, as if unused to such courtesies. Then she linked her arm in his. They strolled across the manicured lawn as it sloped gradually down to the stream that marked the eastern border of the estate. There, underneath an ancient oak tree, the site of so many past picnics, Freddie spread the blanket and Anne unpacked the picnic basket.

Cook had outdone herself. There were sandwiches for Ian and lobster patties for the adults, not to mention biscuits, pastries and fruits fresh from the conservatory. But Freddie could not help feeling a pang of longing for the simpler times in years past when he and Anne had picnicked on this very spot. Then they had dined on whatever scraps they could wheedle from the kitchen, had drunk cold water from the stream, but he recalled the meals as having been fit for royalty. Or perhaps it had not been the food he had enjoyed so much as he had welcomed any chance to escape from his regimented life at Beechwood Park.

No meal could ever compare to the memories of his childhood; still they managed to do justice to the fine meal Cook had provided. Ian, having eaten his fill, and being bored by the adult conversation, stood up and began to investigate the meadow.

Freddie leaned back against the tree, stretching his legs out. He could not remember the last time he had felt this much at peace.

"Be careful, love," Anne called, seeing that Ian was making his way toward the stream. "Don't go too near the edge."

"He'll be fine," Freddie said. The boy was scarce fifty feet away, and at midsummer the stream was so low that a man could easily wade across it. There was little risk of the child coming to harm, although Ian's clothes were bound to become a trifle muddy.

"I sound a fusspot, I know. But I do worry about him. And there is so little I can do to protect him."

She looked at Ian, her expression forlorn. Freddie's throat tightened. He knew she was not talking about the ordinary trials and tribulations of childhood. Anne could not protect her son from the consequences of his birth.

"He seems a fine lad. You have done a good job with him," Freddie said, trying to comfort her.

"He is a darling. But I should never have brought him here. And I never should have taken him to the village this morning. What happened was my fault."

Anger stirred in him as he remembered the events of that morning. "It was not your fault. What happened this morning was regrettable, but it was just one man. You mustn't judge all of New Biddeford by Tom Sweet's example."

Anne shook her head regretfully. "You are being kind, but we both know this is no place for me. As soon as my affairs are in order, Ian and I will be returning home."

"Home? To Canada?" But this was her home. She could not leave. Not now. Not after she'd just returned.

"Nova Scotia, actually. In time Ian will forget all this"—she waved her hand to indicate the estate— "and it will be as it was before."

He reached his arm out as if he could make her stay, and then let it fall as he realized how foolish a gesture it was. Of course Anne wanted to return home. It was perfectly understandable. But a selfish part of him did not want to let her go.

"Permit me to say that I will miss you. It has not been the same without you here. In your absence I have turned into a dreadfully dull fellow," he said, trying to recapture the carefree mood that had vanished with the mention of her present circumstances.

His words had their intended effect, for Anne's

face lost its forlorn look. "You? Dull? Surely you are mocking me."

He glanced over and saw that Ian was busy trying to skip stones across the stream. Reaching into the picnic basket, he withdrew the bottle of wine and a pair of glasses. He made a mental note to stop by the kitchen and thank the Websters' cook for her foresight in including a bottle of wine along with the tamer lemonade.

He handed her one of the newly filled glasses.

"I will tell you the tale, but I warn you it is not a pretty one," he said, his voice heavy with mock irony.

"Pray, speak on," Anne said with equal irony.

Pleased to see that the shadows had left her eyes, he set out to amuse her.

"In my first Season in London, I found myself a young man of no particular distinction. The gentlemen treated me as a younger brother, and the ladies constantly inquired if I should not still be in school somewhere. Since I was all of nineteen this did not distress me, but when I was one and twenty, it became a trifle tedious."

He paused to take a sip of his wine. It was not the time to tell her that he had spent those years secure in the knowledge that one day Anne would return home and that he would claim her. Only gradually had he come to the realization that Anne was not returning and that he would have to set a new course for his life.

"Realizing that I needed to be noticed, I set myself out to become one of the dandy set."

Here he was rewarded by a giggle. "You? A dandy? I can not imagine that."

"Oh, but you must. For years I was a slave to fashion. Patterned waistcoats? I have dozens, each more outrageous than the last. Embroidered silk stockings? I went through them in the hundreds. I spent hours each day contemplating the tying of my cravat, and when the task of keeping up my appearance proved too much for my valet, I hired him an assistant. Really, I can not bear to contemplate the depths of my follies," Freddie said, shuddering in mock horror. He was exaggerating, of course. But only slightly.

"And what happened?"

"Nothing. For all my endeavors, I could not change the opinion of the *ton*. I was still Viscount Frederick, a dull, if worthy gentleman, with a title and income that inspired scheming mamas and fortune hunters. The young ladies themselves found me a convenient escort, but, alas, hardly a romantic figure. Eventually I realized the futility of trying to make myself something that I was not, and I renounced my claim as a dandy." Even he could hear the note of self-pity in his voice. He had meant to amuse her, not make her feel sorry for him.

"I can not believe it was as bad as all that," Anne said.

"But I have not told you the worst of it," Freddie added, compelled to tell her the whole of it. "Did I mention my marriage proposals? For several years I have been seeking a wife. A woman of gentility to satisfy my family, and with a kind heart and affectionate nature to satisfy myself."

"And did you find her?"

"Of course. Not once, but a dozen times." He forced himself to smile, to cover the hurt that he still felt at the memory of those past rejections.

"Each young lady declined the honor of becoming my wife. This season it was Miss Sommersby. An exceptional girl, modest to a fault. She had not even realized I was courting her. But in the end she refused my suit, telling me that she cared for me as a brother."

"Miss Sommersby is an idiot. Any woman would be lucky to have you for a husband," Anne said hotly.

"I appreciate your vote of confidence. Even if you and my mother are the only two females who seem to feel that way," he said. Her ready defense helped ease the sting of his humiliation. "Still, if she hadn't refused me, I might never have felt the urge to rusticate. And then I wouldn't have found you again. So you see, things do work out for the best."

Anne, who had leaned closer while he told his tale, now drew back. "Er, indeed," she said, seemingly flustered. She turned her face away and looked at the picnic basket as if it were an object of great fascination. "These past years, I have often thought of you and how you were faring," she said softly.

Then she lifted her head and forced a teasing smile to her lips. "But I never would have imagined you as a pink of the *ton*. I am sorry that I was not here to see it."

"I am sorry as well." Regret stabbed through him, followed by sorrow over their lost chances, surprising him with a depth of emotion that he had not felt for a very long time.

He could not help thinking how different their lives would have been if Anne had never made that fateful trip. Would they have been married, with children of their own? Or had their course been set even before Anne had left? Had her father banished her to Canada because of her disgrace? And if she had fallen into trouble, why hadn't she confided in him? He would have done anything to help her. Anything. Surely she had known that.

Ian gave a shriek, and Freddie looked over to see that the boy had fallen into the stream. He jumped up, but before he had taken more than a few steps, Ian was standing up in the midst of the stream. He was soaking wet, but he did not appear hurt. In fact he was positively beaming with excitement.

"A giant fish, he's here, I saw him, I did!" Ian shouted; then he bent over and peered closely at the running water. He showed no discomfort over his soaking-wet condition, no inclination to leave the stream.

Mindless of his hessians, Freddie waded into the stream and grabbed the boy by the collar. With a heave he plucked Ian from the waters and deposited him on the bank where Anne stood waiting. She hugged Ian fiercely, then stepped back and looked at him with dismay. "Look at you. You're completely soaked."

"I nearly had him," Ian said. "If he hadn't wiggled, I would have got him for sure."

"You know better than to jump into a stream like that," Anne said. "You frightened me, not to mention Lord Frederick who went in after you."

Ian looked contrite. "I am sorry, Mama. And, Lord Frederick, I am sorry you got all wet. I didn't mean to fall in. It just happened."

Freddie climbed up the bank. His boots were

soaked, not to mention his breeches which were wet to the knees. He and Ian both made a sorry sight.

"It is nothing. But next time, heed your mother and do what she tells you," Freddie said. With a sense of disappointment, he realized that this mishap spelled the end to any chance of private conversation with Anne.

"At least it is a warm day," she observed. "Still, we must get you inside and out of those muddy clothes."

She took Ian back to the oak tree, then wrapped him up in the blanket.

Freddie helped Anne repack the picnic basket, but the mood of intimacy was lost. It was clear that all of Anne's attention was focused on her son. He escorted them back to the house, where Anne gave orders that a hot bath be drawn.

"I will take my leave," he said. "But say that I may call again."

"I would like that," Anne responded with a smile.

And with that he had to be content.

Six

The next morning, Freddie rose early, as was his custom when he was at Beechwood Park. He breakfasted alone, then left the house and headed for the stables. A groom saddled Ajax for him, and Freddie set off on his morning ride.

The dew was still on the grass, and traces of mist lingered in the shade where the sun had not yet reached. The air was cool, but not chilly. This was his favorite time, when all was still and the day seemed full of endless possibilities.

He had no particular destination in mind when he set out, but somehow after a half-hour's riding he found himself on the lane that led to the Websters' residence. On impulse, he decided to see if Anne could be coaxed for a ride.

Anne's butler raised his eyebrows as he realized the identity of the early morning caller, but eventually he agreed to send for his mistress.

Freddie stood there in the entranceway, tapping his crop idly against his boots. He glanced out the window, to assure himself that the footman was indeed walking Ajax in circles so the horse would not cool off. After a brief delay, Anne appeared.

"What on earth are you doing here?" she asked. "Do you know it is not yet eight o'clock?"

He hadn't actually, but now it occurred to him that it was a trifle early for him to be calling. "I came to ask you to join me in a ride," he explained.

"Now?"

"Now," he said. "I know it is incredibly foolish for me to have called, but it is such a beautiful day. I was riding past, and I thought how much you would enjoy this. And then I thought, Why not? And here I am."

"No," she said, shaking her head.

"But why not?"

"I can not."

He shrugged his shoulders philosophically. "I should not have called without warning. But if not today, then perhaps tomorrow. At a civilized hour."

"I am afraid that will not be possible. Not tomorrow or any other day."

He had a sudden flash of understanding. He should have realized it sooner. After all, he had seen the empty stables for himself on his first visit.

"If it is a suitable horse you are lacking, I would be happy to loan you one from my stables," he said.

"It is not that," Anne said, biting her lip. "It is much simpler. I have no riding habit."

He blinked at her, nonplused. "But why not wear one of your old ones? If it is out of fashion, what do you care? There is no one to see."

Her lips tightened. "You did not hear what I said. I said I have *no* riding habit. After he determined that neither I nor Sarah was returning, my late father apparently decided to rid himself of all our possessions. Nothing remains from before. Not a riding habit or gown, not even the books and toys from when we were children."

His cheerful mood was shattered by her revelation. "I am sorry," he said, knowing how inadequate his words were.

He thought for a moment. "I can lend you a horse, and send over one of my sister's habits. You are closest in size to Elizabeth, I think."

"Freddie, you can not give away your sister's garments. Nor can I accept them from you. It is not proper."

"Elizabeth would not mind. I know she would not." When Elizabeth had remarried earlier in the year, she had left behind a substantial wardrobe at Beechwood. Surely there would be a riding habit or two. And if not in Elizabeth's wardrobe, then Priscilla had dozens. He had paid the bills for them himself.

"A lady does not accepts gifts of clothing. Not from a gentleman," Anne repeated. "It is not proper."

He knew from the stubborn set of her jaw that she had made up her mind. But he did not like it. When had Anne developed this overwhelming concern with propriety? There had been a time when she had begged him for the loan of his outgrown breeches and shirt so she could practice riding astride.

Of course that had been many years ago, when Anne had been a skinny girl with nary a curve to be seen. Nowadays, she would make quite a different picture should she appear in breeches and a shirt. Alas, with her newfound concern for propriety it was

unlikely that he would have the chance to see her
in such attire.

"If you will not go riding, then will you agree to
a drive? Tomorrow, perhaps."

She nodded. "I would like that. But please, pick
a civilized hour."

"I will call for you after lunch, if that is agree-
able."

"I look forward to it."

At first he had been disappointed that he would
have to settle for a sedate drive on country lanes, as
opposed to an energetic ride cross-country along the
hunt trails. But by the time he called for her the next
day, he was prepared to enjoy the drive simply because it gave him a chance to be with her.

"Is there anywhere in particular you would like to
see?" he asked, as she settled herself into the carriage.

"I am at your disposal," she said.

Remembering her comments from yesterday, he
was not surprised to see that she was wearing the
same dark brown walking dress she had worn the day
he had seen her in the village. He supposed it could
be called serviceable, although ugly was the first word
that came to his mind. The dress was years out of
fashion, and did nothing to complement Anne's figure or complexion. But he held his tongue, knowing
Anne would not appreciate such a sentiment.

"Let us just see where the road takes us," he said.

He drove her past the home farm, where he had
introduced Ian to jumping. Then he took her past
Sir William Dunne's, so she could glimpse the folly

that the Dunnes had added to their property. Finally, because the day was so fine, he showed her the woods where his workers were harvesting timber, and he explained how, for each tree taken, the workers planted two more to ensure that there would be timber for generations to come.

She seemed genuinely interested, so he began to describe for her his various enterprises. "People see the estate and they think of the tenant farmers or perhaps the home farm," he said. "But it is more than that. There is the timber, the gristmill which serves farmers for miles around, and, of course, the livestock."

"Horses," she said. "You always wanted to raise horses."

He grimaced, thinking of his selection of Ajax. Ajax was a good mount, but Freddie had entirely misread the character of the animal when he chose him. "No, I fear any enterprise that relied upon my skill at choosing horseflesh would be doomed to failure. Our livestock consists of the dairy cows. And soon we will have the goats."

A peal of laughter burst from her. "Oh, Freddie. Goats?"

"Yes, goats. Martin Lansdowne, my agent, has conceived a plan to have the cottagers raise the goats and then sell their wool to a felt manufacturer. Apparently, it is not just any goat hair that is required, but a specific kind of goat."

"I see. Thoroughbred goats, as it were," Anne teased.

"Well, he is seldom wrong about these matters," Freddie said, defending the absent Martin. "In any case I agreed to give it a try, so he's off now, arranging to buy a few dozen of these goats. We'll offer them to any of the tenants who wish to try their hand at goat-rearing, in exchange for a share of the profit from when we sell the wool."

It was a good plan. The end of the long war with Napoleon had brought peace, and a flood of cheap foreign corn flooding into the British markets. This in turn had led to the harsh Corn Laws, which had caused many a landlord and farmer to fall on hard times. Beechwood Park had been spared, in part because they had had the foresight to diversify their interests. If the goat scheme proved successful, it would help diversify them even more.

"I am certain that you would not do this, did you not think it a wise investment. But I can not help picturing you as Frederick, viscount of Goats. You must admit it has a fine ring to it," she teased.

She chuckled, and he began to laugh as well, enjoying the easy camaraderie that made it possible for her to tease him.

They drove on for some moments, until they reached the top of the hill where two lanes intersected. There he turned the carriage around, until they were facing the way they had come. The valley lay spread out before them. From here they could see nearly the whole of the estate. Below them and to the left lay Beechwood Park, with its magnificent gardens and manicured lawns, leading down to the lake. Beyond the lake were the woods and the home farm, and then the tenant farms that stretched to the borders of New Biddeford.

"This is my favorite spot," he explained. "Sometimes, when I am troubled, I will come here and look down into the valley until the world makes sense again."

Anne squeezed his arm in sympathy. "You have a great deal of responsibility," she said. "And you came to it much too young."

He nodded. "I was scarcely older than Ian when my father died, and I became Viscount. Overnight I was responsible for all this," he said, with a wave of his hand. "My mother, my five sisters, Beechwood Park, all our tenants and servants and laborers—all dependent on me. I think you were the only one who understood how frightened I was."

"I know," she said, softly. "But you were trying so hard to be brave that I never let on."

The Dowager Lady Frederick had been determined to instill in her son the traditions of his ancestors. Day and night she had drilled into his head the words that she lived by. Duty. Responsibility. She had no patience for a boy who wept for the father he had lost, or who confessed that he was afraid of being sent away to school. Such weaknesses were for lesser mortals.

But whenever he felt he had too much to bear, he escaped to visit Anne. She expected nothing from him other than his friendship, and offered her friendship in return. She had been the one saving grace during those dark times.

"In those days I think I hated my mother," he confessed. "But because of, or perhaps in spite of, her, I have come to love this place. This is my land, and these are my people. I can think of nowhere else I would rather be, no better way to spend my life than caring for the land and passing it on to my children."

It was all he had ever wanted. All he lacked was a woman to share his life with him.

"This land is all that I ever wanted," he said aloud. "But what is it that you want?"

Anne opened her mouth and then closed it, as if uncertain of what she should say. After a moment's reflection she said just one word.

"Choices," she said.

"Choices? But what would you choose?"

"I do not know," she said. "I envy you, for you have found what you want while I am still looking. But I would like to know that someday, should I find my heart's desire, I would be free to choose."

She must have sensed that he was puzzled, so she tried to explain. "All our life is a series of choices. When you are young, it seems as if the world is before you, and you can do whatever you want. But each choice you make is like a turn on the road, until one day you find your path has narrowed, and there are no more forks in the road. Yet you can not go back."

"I see." He thought he understood. Whatever choices she had made, or had been forced on her, Anne was now an unmarried woman raising a child. Her past transgressions would shape any future that she might have.

He released the brake and shook the reins, and the horse started down the hill. "I wish things could be different," he said.

"So do I," Anne replied. "But I stopped believing in wishes long ago."

Seven

Anne's days settled into a routine. Mornings were devoted to Ian's lessons. After lunch he would be set free to play, under the watchful eyes of Samson or one of the other servants, while Anne supervised the servants who were compiling the household inventory or wracked her brains trying to understand her father's account books. Her father had acted as his own agent, which meant that there was no one who could advise her. And in the last months of his illness, he had neglected much that must now be put to rights.

As she had since her arrival, Anne made a point of stopping her labors each afternoon and joining Ian for tea. If the weather was fair they would go for a stroll, or she would watch him as he played. Occasionally Freddie would join them. He often called without ceremony, just as he had in the old days. But these days he was always accompanied by a groom, and she, mindful of appearances, made certain that there was always a servant to play propriety.

When she was otherwise occupied, Freddie proved himself more than willing to entertain Ian, and the two had formed a fast friendship. They had gone riding on several occasions, and the other day he had taught Ian to fish. The pair had returned muddy but triumphant, bearing three of the smallest fish Anne had ever seen. They had both seemed enormously proud of themselves, and after taking a deep breath to stifle her giggles, she had heaped them with all the praise that the two mighty fishermen seemed to feel they deserved.

If not for Freddie, Anne would have felt truly alone. There were the servants, true, but she could hardly ask their advice or depend upon them for conversation. And although there was no repeat of the earlier scene at the lending library, neither did the villagers go out of their way to befriend her.

She found herself leaning more and more on Freddie's strength. When she was unable to make heads or tails of her father's estate books, he not only lent her the services of his own agent, but spent an entire afternoon patiently going over the books with her.

It was frightening how quickly Freddie had become a necessary part of her world. The days when he did not call seemed unbearably dull. She could not imagine how she had survived without his friendship for all these years. For six years she had sacrificed her own dreams to care for Ian. And though she would make the same choice again, it was only now that she realized just how much she had given up.

And so, knowing that her time here would soon be over, Anne tried to savor each day, to store up memories to last for the years to come.

In the end, her idyll lasted nearly a month. Then,

early one afternoon, Freddie was shown into the drawing room. He smiled as he came in, but his smile seemed forced and quickly faded.

"Your pardon, Miss Webster, but I wonder if I might have a word with you?"

"Of course," she said, wondering at his sudden formality. "Pray, take a seat."

Freddie's eyes flickered toward the maid who had shown him in. "It is a fine day. Perhaps we could stroll outside, to take some air?"

Whatever he wanted to speak to her about, it was something he did not want to say in front of the servants. "I will need but a moment to fetch my bonnet."

She returned, tying the straw bonnet's strings under her chin as Freddie waited patiently by the door. Then he took her by the arm. He led her outside, onto the side lawn. He seemed to have no particular destination in mind, but instead stared fixedly ahead, showing no inclination to speak, though she could feel the tension in his arm. As the silence stretched on, her imagination supplied her with half-a-dozen reasons for his grim mood, each more unlikely than the last.

Finally she could bear it no longer. "Is Lady Frederick well? And your sisters and their families?"

Freddie gave her a quick glance. "Yes, Mother is well, and my sisters were all fine at last report."

"Then what is amiss? Something is troubling you. I can feel it."

He took a deep breath. "I don't know how to tell you this."

"Ian?" Her pulse quickened though logic told her that nothing could have befallen Ian. She had seen him not an hour past, playing with his toy soldiers in his room.

"No, nothing has happened to Ian. But this concerns him."

Anne forced herself to attend his words.

Freddie raked his free hand through his hair, something he did only when he was nervous. He would not meet her eyes.

"I am afraid I have done you a grave disservice," he said. "Only this morning I was informed that the village gossips have now decided that my interest in Ian, is, er, is a fatherly interest." He stopped walking and began kicking at the ground with the toe of his boot. "And there is more. By all accounts, you and I are said to have resumed our illicit relationship."

Freddie's face was scarlet with embarrassment. He looked at her, misery in his eyes. "Anne, I am so sorry. I never meant to add to your troubles."

His words shocked her, but shock quickly turned to anger as she realized the implications of his words. "Those, those sanctimonious prigs!" she exclaimed. "Not content to drag my name in the mire, they must now blacken yours as well."

It was completely unfair. Freddie had done nothing save be kind to her, and now he would suffer for his gallantry.

Freddie blinked, as if uncertain he had heard her correctly. "You do not blame me?"

"Of course not," she said. "You have done nothing wrong, unless friendship is now a crime."

He seemed to relax when he realized that she did not hold him responsible for this. "Still, I am afraid this is partly my fault," he said. "I should have known my frequent visits would set tongues to wagging."

There was some truth to his words. An unmarried woman did not normally entertain gentlemen callers. Certainly not while she was living alone, without any chaperone or female relative to lend her countenance. But this was not an ordinary circumstance. She and Freddie had been friends for most of their lives. And they had not exchanged so much as an improper glance, let alone conducted an illicit affair.

"I suppose it does not matter that we have done nothing wrong," she said. "Appearances are all, and character matters for naught. Why is it that so many prefer to believe the worst of others?"

She was no longer surprised about the gossip concerning herself, but how dare they accuse Freddie? She felt herself shaking with fury. Freddie gathered her hands in his and gave them a brief squeeze of reassurance.

Then he linked arms, and they began to walk again.

"If you think it best, I will not call here any longer," he said.

"No," she said quickly. "Do not stay away for my sake. The damage is done, and what we do now will not change their minds," she explained. She would not let malicious gossip deprive her of his friendship.

He nodded. "I had come to the same conclusion," he said. "But there must be something I can do to put things right. Name the deed, and it is done."

Anne knew he was sincere in his offer, but there was nothing he could do to set things right. She knew from bitter experience that people believed what they wanted to believe.

"Even if we told the truth about Ian's birth, I doubt that anyone would believe it. My own father did not."

Freddie raised his eyebrows, but true gentleman that he was, he did not ask the question that she knew was uppermost in his mind. She hesitated, having been long used to keeping her own counsel. Still it would be good to unburden herself, and now that he had been dragged into this, Freddie deserved to know the truth.

She took a deep breath, as she thought how best to begin. "My first Season did not go smoothly, as you know. It seems I was always putting my foot wrong. I was too young, I daresay, and soon earned a reputation as a hoyden. So when my sister Sarah wrote, saying how lonely she was, and how much she would like a visit from me, my father saw it as the answer to his prayers."

Even now she could remember how puzzled she had been by her sister's request. She and Sarah had entirely opposite temperaments. Even as children they had never been close. But a trip to Canada had seemed such an adventure that Anne had not protested the planned visit. Who could have known it was not a visit but exile that awaited her there?

She forced herself to continue. "When I arrived, I found Sarah was embroiled in scandal. To make a long story short, she was five months pregnant, and it was widely known that the child was not her husband's."

Freddie drew a sharp breath. "Indeed," he said.

"Indeed." There was no need to tell him the full

depths of Sarah's disgrace. Sarah had developed quite a reputation at the provincial capital. She was rumored to have had numerous lovers, but the rumors did not turn to open scandal until it was known she was pregnant.

"Sarah died giving birth to Ian. Her husband, Colonel Fitzwilliam, told everyone that the baby had been stillborn. I suppose he wanted to put the whole mess behind him. The colonel would have sent Ian to an orphanage, but I could not bear that. I took Ian myself, and wrote to my father to tell him the news."

"But then, why the secrecy? Why did you not return home?"

"Because my dear father did not believe me," Anne said, trying but failing to keep her tone light. "He thought the sun rose and set on Sarah. He accused me of giving birth to a bastard child and of trying to take advantage of Sarah's death to save my own reputation."

And here her reputation had hurt her, for it was Anne Webster who was known to have a wild streak, while her sister Sarah was the model of propriety. Sarah had never put a foot wrong in her entire life, or so her father had believed.

"But how could he?" The outrage in his voice comforted her.

"Perhaps this was easier for him than to think ill of his beloved Sarah. Whatever his reasons, he forbid me to return home. I would have been in desperate straits indeed if Colonel Fitzwilliam had not intervened. He settled an allowance on me and found me a place to live. I called myself Mrs. Webster, told the villagers that I was the widow of an ensign in the colonel's regiment. We would be living there quietly still, if my father hadn't decided to send for us."

It sounded more generous than it was. In exchange for Colonel Fitzwilliam's assistance, Anne had promised not to reveal to anyone the true circumstances of Ian's birth. It was only with Ian's inheritance that she had been freed from her dependence upon the colonel and could thus confide in Freddie.

She could see Freddie considering the implications of her story.

"Your father must have realized his mistake," he said. "After all, he did send for you. And he changed his will in favor of Ian."

"Yes, and named me as one of Ian's guardians. But there, too, he did me no favors, for he made no reference to Sarah. Till the end, I think he believed that Ian was my child and not hers."

She had told herself that it did not matter, but her father's opinions still had the power to hurt her, even after his death. No matter that reason told her her father had been a bitter old man who had robbed himself of the chance to enjoy his daughter and his grandchild. Reason could not overrule her heart, which still ached for the approval that he had never given her and that now would never come.

As he listened to her recount the story, he felt anger at how shabbily she had been treated. But mixed with the anger was a thread of joy and relief. Anne was innocent. Had been innocent all this time. He had imagined a hundred scenarios, with Anne as the victim of seduction or ravishment. But he had never guessed that the truth was the simplest of all.

Ian, dearly loved though he was, was not Anne's child.

He felt ashamed that he had ever doubted her, even for a single moment. He should have trusted his heart. Anne was as she had always been, honorable, affectionate and loyal to a fault. And far too impulsive for her own good. It was like her to promise to care for Ian first and only later to stop and consider the consequences of her decision.

"I have always known you were kind, but I never knew how brave you were," he said. Mere words were inadequate to express how he felt. Anne had taken on the burden of her sister's shame, for the sake of the orphaned child. He could not even begin to guess what that had cost her.

"I don't feel brave at all. Just weary."

Anne's face was white and set, and she was blinking back tears. Freddie longed to put his arms around her, to comfort her, but he did not, being all too conscious that they were in full view of anyone in the house. He had done enough harm to her reputation already. He contented himself with giving her hand a quick squeeze.

"Does Ian know?"

"He knows that his mother died when he was born, and that she asked me to raise him. I will wait until he is older to tell him the rest. And no, I do not know who his real father was. Nor do I wish to."

They continued walking till they reached the marble bench that marked the end of the path. Anne seated herself on the bench, but Freddie remained standing. He could not sit. His mind could not grasp the enormity of what Anne had endured for the sake of her family. Nor could he find a way to vent his rage. Her callous father was dead, beyond any earthly punishment. And even if she told her story, without proof who would believe her? She would only be exposing herself to ridicule and scorn.

"I think it would be best if I left here now," Anne said, after a moment of reflection. "I had booked passage home in September, but I am certain I can find an earlier sailing. Between them, your agent and Mr. Creighton can attend to the details of the estate. And when I am gone, the gossip will die down as well. Your reputation should suffer no lasting harm."

"I do not care about the gossip." He did not care what they said about him. And he did not want her to leave. Anne deserved better than to be driven out of the county by malicious gossips. But how could he possibly convince her to stay? There was nothing for her here, unless . . .

"Promise me that you will hear me out. I know how we can put an end to the gossip and ensure that you and Ian can remain here in England, where you belong."

Anne gazed at him skeptically. "And how would you accomplish this miracle?"

"Marry me."

"Have you lost your mind?"

It was not the response he had been hoping for. Still she hadn't laughed at him or, worse yet, said she regarded him merely as a brother.

"It is a logical solution. We have always gotten along well together, have we not? I need a wife, you need a husband and Ian needs a father."

Anne shook her head. "It is not logical at all. Your

offer does you great credit, but you can not go around offering to marry girls out of pity."

"It is not pity," he said, angry that she should think so little of herself. "You are good-hearted, loyal, affectionate and willing to put up with all my foibles. What more could a man ask for in a wife?"

It all seemed so clear to him. Why could she not see it as well?

Anne bit her lip, and he could tell she was wavering.

"Come now, say yes," he urged. "Nine years ago you promised me that we would marry as soon as we were both of age. And here we are, older if no wiser. What say we make a match of it?"

She smiled, and for a moment he thought she was about to agree, but then his heart dropped as he heard the dreaded word.

"No," she repeated. "I am honored, but we both know that this can never be. It will be seen as the confirmation of the rumors. Your family will never accept me, and Ian would grow up on the fringes of society, an outcast because of his birth."

"It wouldn't be like that," he argued, even though a part of him knew she was right. He felt helpless. He would have slain a dozen dragons for Anne, but it seemed there was nothing he could do to save her from her current predicament.

"And lastly, you deserve to marry a woman that you love, one who loves you in return."

"But of course I love you." Didn't she realize that?

"Yes. As a friend."

He argued, but she stood firm. In the end, all he could win was her promise that she would consider his offer.

* * *

As Freddie approached the gates that led to Beechwood Park, his spirits were downcast. Learning of Anne's innocence should have gladdened his heart. And indeed there was a part of him that had rejoiced upon realizing that Ian was not the product of Anne's love for another. But her innocence did not change her circumstances. Freddie knew the truth; others did not. He understood why she felt she must leave. He did not want her to go, yet if she did not agree to his proposal, she would soon be gone from his life forever.

If he truly loved her, how could he ask her to stay? Even with the protection of his name, it might take years before the marriage was accepted by his family and by society. If it had been just Anne, Freddie was sure he could have convinced her. But there was Ian to consider. Freddie had grown fond of the boy. It would be a privilege to stand as father for him, but was that in Ian's best interests? Or would Ian be better served by a childhood spent in obscurity, where none knew his connections?

Freddie guided Ajax past the house and toward the stable block. There he found the yard bustling with activity. A livery coach stood in the yard, surrounded by boxes and trunks of every size and description. A steady stream of footmen were engaged in carrying the luggage inside. Beyond the livery coach was an elegant traveling carriage and beyond that what appeared to be a carters' wagon. It, too, was filled with trunks that were being unloaded by the grooms.

Good lord, Priscilla must have bought out half of London, Freddie thought.

Fortunately the commotion did not bother Ajax. Freddie dismounted, and a moment later one of the grooms noticed him and came running over.

"Sorry, my lord, but as you can see, we're at sixes and sevens here."

Freddie nodded. "I take it my sister has returned?"

"Yes, my lord. Just down from London."

He wondered why his mother hadn't reminded him that Priscilla was returning on this day. Then, again, he had given her little opportunity to do so. That morning, when his mother had mentioned the latest gossip about Anne, Freddie had stormed out of the house without so much as a by-your-leave.

As the groom led Ajax away, Freddie heard a loud crash, followed by the sound of a man cursing. Turning he saw the cause of the excitement; one of the footmen had apparently dropped a trunk on the toes of another. The injured footman made a pathetic sight, clutching his injured foot in one hand while he reviled the guilty party with every curse word he knew. "You clumsy bastard! You're nothing but a mangy scum—"

"His lordship!" a dozen voices hissed.

The footman turned and, seeing Freddie, took his hand off his foot, straightening up and then wincing as the injured member touched the ground. "Beg your pardon, sir."

"I heard nothing. Carry on," Freddie said.

He entered the house by the side door, and made his way to his rooms to change. The house, which had seemed so empty just this morning, now teemed with activity. He heard servants passing up and down the halls, delivering luggage, fetching water for washing and attending to a dozen errands.

He was glad that Priscilla was home, though he was in no mood to hear about her triumphs in London. He knew she was merely high-spirited, but at times his sister made him feel as old as Methuselah. Still, for her sake he would try to be cheerful and would feign an interest in all she had seen and done since last he saw her.

There was some consolation in knowing that Priscilla's arrival meant that Elizabeth must be here as well. Of all his sisters, Freddie felt closest to Elizabeth. Perhaps because she was nearest to him in age, or maybe it was simply her calm good sense. Whatever the reason, he had need of her counsel now.

Freddie left his room, and made his way to the Blue Room, where his mother preferred to receive family. As he entered the room, Priscilla squealed with delight, then jumped up from her chair.

He had only a second to brace himself before she threw herself at him. Wrapping her arms around him, she exclaimed, "Oh, Freddie, I have missed you so."

He gave her a squeeze and then unwrapped her arms from around his neck. "Now, puss, let me get a look at you."

He took a step back and pretended to study her critically. "Hmmm, have you gotten taller since I saw you last? And what is this, a freckle?" he asked, tapping her nose with one finger.

"A freckle? Oh, no." She rushed to the mirror that stood over the fireplace. Examining her com-

plexion, she realized at once that he was teasing her.
"You beast!" she said.

Freddie chuckled. Priscilla would never change.
He crossed the room to where Elizabeth and her
husband, Mr. David Rutledge, stood. He kissed his
sister on the cheek, and shook hands with his
brother-in-law.

"Welcome to Beechwood Park," he said. "I am so
pleased that you could join us."

"Thank you," Mr. Rutledge replied. "Elizabeth
has told me so much about her former home that
I feel I already know the place."

Freddie took the opportunity to study the man
who had won his sister's heart. Cruelly widowed in
the first year of her marriage, Elizabeth had spent
the next six years mourning her first husband. But
then she had met David Rutledge, and he had
coaxed her out of her solitude. Within a week of
their meeting, she had discarded her somber gowns
and thrown away the caps that had added ten years
to her age.

They had been married just three months before,
and from the quiet happiness on Elizabeth's face,
Freddie could see that she was well pleased with her
choice.

"I hope you did not find Priscilla too much of a
handful," he said.

Elizabeth and David Rutledge exchanged a private
glance and conspiratorial smiles. "Priscilla was a perfect angel," Elizabeth assured him.

For their sakes he hoped it was not too much of
an exaggeration.

Priscilla chose this moment to enter the conversation. "I can not wait until my ball. I invited simply

dozens of my friends. If they all come, it will be a
sad crush indeed."

Dozens? Surely he had misheard. He heard the
door open behind him.

Priscilla took a deep breath. She had the gleam
in her eye that meant she was up to one of her
schemes. "And, of course, there was one particular
friend who journeyed with us from London. She did
not know if she should come, but I told her you
would be pleased to see her."

"Any friend of yours is welcome," Freddie said
automatically. He turned to greet the new arrival.

His jaw dropped, and he stood for a moment in
stunned silence.

"Miss Sommersby."

"Lord Frederick." Her voice squeaked as she said
his name.

Time seemed to stand still. He waited for the earth
to swallow him up. He could not imagine anything
more awkward than being forced to entertain the
woman who had rejected his offer of marriage.

Freddie glanced around. Priscilla looked defiant,
and he realized at once what must have happened.
Priscilla, along with the rest of London, had known
that he was courting Miss Sommersby. He hadn't
told Priscilla that he had offered marriage to Miss
Sommersby and been refused. There had seemed
no reason to tell his sister—except now the minx
had taken it into her head to promote the match.

But what was Miss Sommersby's role in all this?
All she had had to do was refuse the invitation. Instead she had come here, and placed them all in
this awkward muddle.

"Miss Sommersby, come sit by me," Elizabeth said,

sensing the undercurrents in the room. "I understand you are from the Lake District. We recently traveled there, and I am certain we must have mutual acquaintances."

As Elizabeth set about entertaining their guest, Freddie let himself be drawn into conversation with his brother-in-law. But only part of his mind was on the conversation, as the rest was focused on his predicament. He could see no escape. It was going to be the longest fortnight of his life.

Eight

After his initial meeting with Miss Sommersby, Freddie managed to get through the rest of that evening without any further awkwardness.

Priscilla attempted to throw the two of them together, suggesting that Freddie conduct Miss Sommersby on a tour of the portrait gallery. When that scheme failed, she next suggested that Freddie partner Miss Sommersby at cards after dinner. Only quick thinking enabled Freddie to sidestep these schemes without making it obvious that he wished to avoid Miss Sommersby's company.

If Priscilla continued to play matchmaker, it would be a long fortnight indeed. He needed to speak with her privately to convince her to end her meddling. But there had been no opportunity to do so last night.

Rising early the next morning, Freddie discovered Mr. Rutledge was also an early riser. An invitation for a morning ride turned into an impromptu tour of the park. Mr. Rutledge said little, but when he did speak his questions were intelligent, and he seemed genuinely interested in Freddie's plans for improving the estate. More importantly, he did not feel compelled to fill every moment with idle chatter. Freddie's opinion of his new brother-in-law rose a notch. He had had little opportunity to get to know Mr. Rutledge in London, but the more he learned of him, the more he understood why Elizabeth had chosen him.

Returning to the house from the stables, he saw Priscilla and Miss Sommersby had chosen to stroll in the rose garden. For a moment he contemplated turning back, but it was too late. Priscilla raised her hand in greeting, and he knew he had no choice but to go forward.

"Blast," Freddie said quietly.

Mr. Rutledge raised his eyebrows inquiringly, but said nothing.

Freddie did not offer an explanation. Mr. Rutledge could draw his own conclusions. As they approached the two women, Freddie arranged his features into a semblance of a smile.

"Good morning, ladies," he said, with a bow. The bow was for the sake of Miss Sommersby. Younger sisters did not rate such courtesies, but as host he had appearances to hold up. He could not help wishing that Priscilla had chosen another young woman as her companion. Any other woman, or even a brace of giggling girls, would have been preferable to having to face the woman who had scorned him only weeks before.

"How fortunate for us that we saw you," Priscilla said, in a tone of voice that was much too sweet to be sincere. "Mr. Rutledge, Elizabeth was looking for you only moments ago. I believe she is still in the morning room."

Mr. Rutledge made his excuses, leaving Freddie alone with the two girls. But not for long.

"Oh, dear," Priscilla said, wrinkling her brow in apparent distaste. "I have only just recalled that I promised Mama I would check to make certain all is in readiness for the guests who will be arriving this weekend, but I dislike having to cut short our stroll."

"We can return later, or on another day," Miss Sommersby offered obligingly.

"No, this is such a beautiful day, and you are here as our guest. I am certain that my brother would be pleased to bear you company in my absence."

Priscilla dimpled up at him, the picture of innocence. Freddie fought the urge to strangle her. He knew perfectly well that their mother would not entrust such a task to the flighty Priscilla. Their formidable housekeeper, Mrs. Braddock, ensured that the house was ready at all times for guests. If the Prince Regent himself were to call, remote as that possibility might be, he would find Beechwood Park was ready to receive him on an instant's notice.

But Priscilla had him trapped, and they both knew it. He could not call his sister a bold-faced liar. At least not while Miss Sommersby looked on.

Nor could he abandon Miss Sommersby to her own devices. As her host, and as a gentleman, Freddie knew what was expected. And he always did what was expected of him.

"Miss Sommersby, I would be happy to offer my escort," he said, with all the enthusiasm of a prisoner facing the gallows. He hoped she would take the hint, but she did not.

"You are most kind," she said.

Miss Sommersby resumed walking, and he fell into step beside her. Her appearance, as always, was flawless. Her sprigged muslin gown not only displayed her figure to advantage, but was the precise shade of blue to match her eyes. In one hand she carried a parasol, which she twirled absentmindedly. Freddie was certain there were dozens, if not hundreds, of young gentlemen who would be delighted to exchange places with him.

Unfortunately none of those gentlemen appeared.

They strolled along the marble path that wound around the garden. Originally a rose garden, over the years Lady Frederick had enlarged it, adding beds of rare flowers and surrounding the whole with herbaceous borders. Each bed mixed flowers of different seasons, so from early spring till late autumn there was always something in bloom or about to bloom.

It fell to Freddie to break the silence. "Did my sister tell you anything of the history of this garden?"

Miss Sommersby shook her head.

"This garden was laid out over one hundred years ago, when my ancestor married a Frenchwoman named Marie Claire. As part of her dowry, she brought with her rosebushes from her family's estate in Provence. The roses in the north bed, and those along the wall are said to be descendants of the first roses that she planted."

"Indeed," she said.

"Over the years, each viscountess has chosen to add to the garden in her own way. My mother prides herself on her ability to cultivate the rarest varieties of flowers," he continued. "Over on the left you can

see the Chinese asters, while on the right we have
Peruvian marigolds."

Or were those the marigolds on the left and the
asters on the right? It did not matter. Miss Sommersby barely glanced at the flowers. She looked as
uncomfortable as he felt.

"Miss Sommersby, if you wish to cut short our
walk, I will not be offended."

She hung her head, and said, "You must wonder
why I came here."

Honesty told him to reply yes, while politeness argued that he say no. So he said nothing.

"I did not wish to. I meant to say no. But your
sister Priscilla was so insistent that before I quite
knew what happened, I found I had agreed to come.
And, of course, after my parents had accepted, I
could hardly say no."

His eyes narrowed in suspicion. Could this be
true? But then, one of the qualities he had admired
in Miss Sommersby had been her compliant nature.

"When my sister gets an idea in her head, it can
be difficult to stand against her," Freddie replied.
"I believe she has some thoughts of matchmaking."

Miss Sommersby blushed, a delicate pink that
served only to emphasize the purity of her complexion. "I don't—I wouldn't—I mean, I certainly,
hope . . ." she stammered.

"Never mind," Freddie said. "Priscilla will soon
lose interest in this scheme and turn her mind to
another. All we need do is remain civil, but show no
partiality toward each other."

"If that is what you want."

The hairs on the back of his neck prickled. "Is
that not what you want as well?"

"Of course," she said, nodding her head vigorously.

But something about her too quick agreement made him deeply uneasy. He wondered just what had happened to Edward Farquhar, whom she had declared her soul mate. Had Farquhar shown his true colors at last? If so, was she here to mend her broken heart? Or because she saw in him a salve for her wounded pride?

He offered to continue the tour, but Miss Sommersby claimed a headache, and so he escorted her back to the side entrance. But he declined to go inside himself. Instead he made his way over past the stables and into the estate yard.

Beechwood House was where the family lived, but the estate yard was the heart of Beechwood Park. Here lay the sawmill, the carpenter's shed, the gardener's bothy, the smithy and all the workshops for the various craftsmen. From an office in the center of the yard, his agent supervised the hundreds of laborers and tenant farmers who comprised the estate.

Martin Lansdowne, the agent, was off touring two of the smaller estates that lay outside the county. He was not due to return for another week, at which time he would bring with him the goats for their newest enterprise.

Freddie spent the morning in the agent's office, attending to the correspondence that had piled up in his absence. He authorized payments of accounts, signed a contract for the sale of corn and inspected catalogs of the latest scientific agricultural instruments.

It was all work that had to be done. But Freddie

knew that he had not come here out of a sense of duty. No, he was simply avoiding his guests. It was a cowardly impulse, but he did not know what else to do. And he doubted Priscilla would think to look for him in here.

Although if she did find him, he would have a word with his sister and set her right. That is, assuming that she was not accompanied by her new friend.

In the end it was Elizabeth who found him.

"Freddie, is there something amiss? I could not believe it when Braddock told me I could find you here."

Freddie waved the seed catalog he held in his hand. "I am reading," he said.

"In here? When you have a perfectly good study of your own? Not to mention the library or the dozens of other public rooms."

He smiled sheepishly. "Very well, you have caught me out. If you must know, I was hoping to avoid another tête-à-tête with Miss Sommersby. Priscilla seems determined to throw the two of us together, and I am running out of excuses to avoid her."

Elizabeth nodded, as if his words had confirmed her own suspicions. "So that is why she invited Miss Sommersby. I thought it odd, since she had never seemed to be a particular friend of Priscilla's before. But there seemed no reason to refuse."

He put the catalog down on the desk and began to fiddle with a pen. "There is more to the situation than meets the eye. Before I left London, I asked Miss Sommersby if she would do me the honor of becoming my wife. She declined."

His sister's eyes opened wide with astonishment.

"Why how perfectly dreadful. And how ill mannered of her to have come here. Does the girl have no sense at all?"

"She claims to find the situation as awkward as I do," Freddie said.

Elizabeth snorted indignantly. "Then she needn't have come." She paused for a moment before continuing, "Unless you wished her to come, that is? Were you dreadfully disappointed when she refused you?"

"No," he said, shaking his head. "She wounded my pride, but that was all. It did not take me long to realize that she had done me a great service by refusing me."

He could no longer remember the impulse that had led him to propose marriage to Miss Sommersby. Why on earth had he ever imagined that he would be satisfied by a marriage of convenience? Especially to such a weak-willed woman as Miss Sommersby had proven herself to be.

"Well, if it is any comfort to you, there was no gossip of this in London. I do not think Priscilla or anyone else knew that you had made an offer to Miss Sommersby." Again she paused for a moment. "I must say, I think less of Miss Sommersby for having accepted the invitation."

"There is more. It seems Mother has lent a hand, inviting Miss Sommersby's parents. They arrive this weekend," Freddie said neutrally.

He did not need to elaborate. His sister could see the implications as well as he. There were many who would see the particular attention paid to Miss Sommersby and her parents' arrival as signs that he was courting the young woman in earnest. And even if he managed to quash Priscilla's schemes, there was his mother to contend with. Miss Sommersby was precisely the sort of young woman the Dowager Lady Frederick would like to see her son take to wife. It was one of the reasons why he had chosen her, after all. He could count on his mother doing everything in her power to promote the match.

"Perhaps it would be best if you went to London for a few days. Mama will be angry, but this will make it clear that Miss Sommersby is here simply as Priscilla's friend and not as your guest."

"No, that is not possible." It was good advice, but he could not leave Anne. Not when there was so much that lay unfinished between them.

"Then what can I do to help?"

"Once the other guests arrive, it will be less awkward. But for now, just stay close and see that Priscilla does not shirk her duty to entertain Miss Sommersby."

"Of course. And you can count on David to do his part."

Freddie took a deep breath, then looked away. "There is one more thing you can do for me. Anne Webster has returned, and she could use a friend."

Elizabeth raised her eyebrows. "Mama mentioned her return in her last letter. She seemed to hint there was some sort of scandal?"

Freddie winced. He did not want to know what his mother had written. He only hoped that she had had the common sense to keep her suspicions within the family rather than broadcasting them to her wide circle of acquaintances.

"I do not care what Mother has written, or what gossip you may have heard. All I ask is that you not

judge Anne until you have seen her for yourself."
If Anne agreed to become his wife, he would need
Elizabeth's support to make her feel welcome.

If Elizabeth guessed at the reason for his request,
she did not say so. "If you ask it of me, then of
course I will go," she responded.

"You have a visitor," Boswell said, extending a sil-
ver tray toward her. Anne wondered who it could
be. In recent weeks she had had no callers, except
for Freddie and the solicitor Mr. Creighton.

Anne picked up the cream-colored card from off
the tray. She turned it over and read the name en-
graved upon it. Mrs. David Rutledge. Strange, she
did not know anyone named Rutledge.

"Shall I tell her you are not at home?"

Anne hesitated. In the first weeks of her return,
several of the ladies from the neighborhood had
called on her, with the express purpose of condemn-
ing her for her scandalous ways or to urge her to
leave the neighborhood at once.

But once the initial shock of her presence had
worn off, the callers had ceased to appear.

"No. Please ask her to join me." Mrs. Rutledge
could be another of their ilk, but Anne would not
be the first to show discourtesy.

Boswell bowed and left, returning a moment later.
"Mrs. David Rutledge," he announced.

"Miss Webster. How good of you to see me. I hope
I am not intruding?"

Mrs. Rutledge was an elegant woman, dressed in
what was presumably the height of London fashion.
She was past her first youth, but could be no more

than thirty. Her face was familiar. Anne felt that she
had seen this woman before, but could not remember where or when.

"Not at all," Anne said. "Please, have a seat and
let me ring for refreshments."

Mrs. Rutledge selected a chair and then sat down,
arranging her skirts with practiced ease.

"You have changed a great deal, I must say. I
would hardly have known you," she said.

"And you have changed as well," Anne said. Who
the devil was this woman? "I must beg your pardon,
but I don't recall where we met."

The woman gave a peal of laughter. "Don't you
recognize me? My name is Rutledge now, but it was
Pennington. Elizabeth Pennington."

Anne blushed, feeling foolish. How could she not
have recognized Freddie's oldest sister? Her only excuse was that she had not seen Elizabeth in years.
Not since Elizabeth's wedding to the dashing Lieutenant Carson.

"I did not know you had remarried," Anne said.
"May I offer you my congratulations?"

"Thank you," Elizabeth Rutledge said. "We were
married only this spring. My new husband is quite
different from my first; nonetheless, I adore him
dreadfully." Her lips curved up in a knowing smile.

"And your daughter, she is well also?"

"Mary is quite well. She is spending the summer
with Lieutenant Carson's family at Brighton. She is
all of seven now, can you imagine?"

Anne felt a sudden stab of envy. Elizabeth Rutledge was everything that she was not. Elegant, confident, secure of her place in society and apparently
happy in her new marriage.

Mrs. Rutledge must know the gossip concerning Anne. Every soul within fifty miles surely had heard it by now. Yet why had she risked her own reputation to call on the supposed sinner? There was no thread of past friendship to bind them together. They had been neighbors, true, but Mrs. Rutledge had been Sarah's friend, not Anne's.

It made no sense, unless she had decided that it was her duty to warn Anne off. Anne braced herself, certain that at any moment Mrs. Rutledge would begin asking probing questions or hinting that it would be best for Anne to leave and to break all connection to the Pennington family.

Instead Mrs. Rutledge chatted easily about past acquaintances, her recent visit to London and her hopes that Mr. Rutledge would find an estate to their liking somewhere near her family. Anne's face grew still, wondering if this was Mrs. Rutledge's way of hinting that the family was willing to buy the Manor, in effect to pay Anne to leave the neighborhood.

But her guest, perhaps sensing Anne's mood, added quickly that she had no wish to settle right on her mother's doorstep, as it were.

The half-hour flew by, and as Mrs. Rutledge rose to leave, Anne realized that she still did not know the purpose of her visit.

"I thank you for your kind hospitality," Mrs. Rutledge said. "I do hope I may call again."

By custom Mrs. Rutledge should have invited Anne to call on her at Beechwood Park, but Anne was not surprised to find that no such invitation was forthcoming.

"Perhaps, next time, you will introduce me to your son," Mrs. Rutledge said.

"Perhaps." But not until she was certain that Mrs. Rutledge bore them no ill will. Anne had learned that lesson at the lending library. She would not make the same mistake twice.

Anne escorted her guest to the entranceway. As Mrs. Rutledge put on her bonnet and collected her parasol, Anne found she could contain her curiosity no longer. "Tell me, why did you decide to call?"

Mrs. Rutledge smiled. "Because my brother asked it of me." And then she left, leaving Anne staring gape-mouthed at her back.

Nine

By Friday the house was full of guests, and Freddie was at his wit's end. He'd hoped that having so many guests would make it easier for him to avoid Miss Sommersby; instead, it seemed everyone present was conspiring to throw them together.

In addition to Miss Sommersby and her parents, there were no less than a dozen ladies and gentlemen who were particular friends of Priscilla's. It should have been easy for him to avoid Miss Sommersby. But the ladies, as always, showed little interest in Freddie, instead preferring to flirt with the other gentlemen present. And those gentlemen treated Miss Sommersby with careful politeness, though there was a marked lack of flirtatiousness in their manner.

It was as if Miss Sommersby wore a sign around her neck, one which read Intended Property of Viscount Frederick. Worse yet, there was nothing he could do about it. He could hardly announce to the assembled guests that he had no interest in Miss Sommersby. Such a declaration would only make him look foolish and would merely serve to add fuel to the rumors.

So he was careful to divide his attention equally among the ladies present. He partnered Miss Glavine at whist, turned the pages for Lady Alice as she played at the pianoforte, and admired the sisters Crane as they sketched the lake. But his scruples went for naught. Miss Glavine developed a headache, and asked dear Miss Sommersby to take her place. Lady Alice declared that her hand had a cramp, and pleaded that only Miss Sommersby could take her place at the instrument.

It wasn't till the day at the lake that he realized the extent of the conspiracy surrounding him. The sisters Crane, good-hearted but none too subtle, spent nearly a quarter-hour discussing the virtues of Miss Sommersby, until Freddie was ready to scream with frustration. And then, seemingly out of nowhere, Miss Sommersby appeared. At once the Crane sisters decided that nothing would do save to have Freddie row Miss Sommersby out on the lake so they could sketch the couple together.

Freddie felt ill. Miss Sommersby blushed and demurred, but then declared that she was only too happy to oblige her friends. Before he knew it, he found himself in the middle of the lake with the one woman he had most hoped to avoid.

He had to admit that Miss Sommersby made a pretty picture as she sat across from him, a parasol shading her from the sun. Freddie bent his back to the oars. He wished for a sudden storm or perhaps a bolt of lightning. Any excuse to cut short this farce. Then again, the way his luck was running, in a storm the boat would capsize, and as a gentleman he would have to save her. Once having saved her life, it would be impossible to convince anyone that he held her in no special regard.

Freddie sighed.

"Is there something wrong, my lord?"

"Tell me, why did you agree to this?"

"Why not? I have always liked boating, and the Misses Crane seemed to have their hearts set on the sketch. It would be unkind to disappoint them."

It was not possible that she could be so naive.

"I did not mean the lake. I meant why did you come here?"

She bit her lip and then bent her head, so that she was looking up at him through lowered lashes. "My lord? I thought I had explained that to you. I didn't mean to come, but your sister insisted . . ."

He gave her a hard look. Miss Sommersby was too amiable for her own good, or a better actress than he had guessed. She had come to Beechwood Park because Priscilla had insisted. No doubt, if he asked, she would have a perfectly innocent explanation for each of the occurrences that had bothered him.

Strange, that it seemed the only time she had ever had the courage to disappoint anyone was when she had refused his offer.

It was time for some plain speaking. "Miss Sommersby, I am certain that you must find this situation as awkward as I do. I do not wish to give offense, but perhaps it would be less trying for both of us if you were to make an effort to avoid my company."

"I never meant for this . . . I mean, if you wish I will leave at once, although what I will tell Mama and Papa I do not know . . ." Her voice broke, and tears sparkled in her eyes.

She looked completely miserable, and he felt like an ogre. He supposed it was the legacy of having four younger sisters, but the sight of a young lady in tears always brought out his protective side.

"No, no. I am not asking you to leave. You and your parents are welcome to stay, till after Priscilla's ball." It was only another five days till the ball. How much trouble could five days be? "But, please, in the future it would be best if you did not seek out my company," he said.

"Thank you," she said tremulously.

"Now be a good girl, and try to smile. You don't want your likeness done with a frown on your face."

Miss Sommersby gave a wan smile. "Of course," she said.

Looking at her, Freddie felt a hundred years old. What had he ever seen in this child? Miss Sommersby had no backbone at all. She could not stand up for herself in the least; the slightest reproof brought her to tears. Marriage to her would have meant a lifetime of soothing her sensibilities and apologizing for imagined offenses.

And he could not imagine anyone more unlike Anne. With Anne, a fellow always knew where he stood. Anne was incapable of saying yes when she meant no, or of agreeing that something was white when all present could see that it was black. Anne never could have found herself in this situation, or if she had, she would have put an abrupt end to the speculation by declaring that she would rather wed a toad than spend one more minute in the hapless gentleman's company.

He smiled, well able to picture the scene in his mind. If only Miss Sommersby had one-tenth of Anne's strength of character. If she had, he might have found himself more in sympathy with her. But as it was, he counted the minutes until he could honorably call an end to the excursion and free himself from her company.

By the time the sketching session was over, Freddie felt he had more than done his duty as host for the day. Appointing David Rutledge to keep an eye on Priscilla and her admirers, Freddie rode over to see Anne.

This was only the second time he had been able to see her since the start of the house party. He was aware that his visits were still cause for gossip, but reasoned that the gossip would continue whether he saw Anne or not. And with any luck, Elizabeth's visit might remind everyone of the closeness that had always existed between the two families.

On his visits he was careful not to press Anne for an answer. He knew if he rushed her, the answer would be no. So he was patient, knowing in time that she would realize all the benefits marriage to him would bring.

When he arrived, Anne seemed pleased to see him. With only a little prompting on her part, he found himself relating the events of the last days.

"And there I was, stuck in the rowboat with that silly girl. I found myself praying for a sudden storm, or for the boat to spring a leak. Even an attack by a lake monster would have been a welcome diversion."

"Poor Freddie," Anne said, but then she spoiled the effect by laughing.

"It is not funny," he insisted.

"A lake monster? Come now. Next you'll be saying that you declared yourself lake-sick, and insisted the girl row you back to shore."

He smiled in spite of himself. "I hadn't thought of that."

"More tea?"

"No, thank you." He put his cup and saucer down on the table and then leaned back against the sofa and stretched his legs out in front of him. For the first time in days he felt himself at peace.

"I do not understand her," he said. "At times, I think she is as mortified by the situation as she claims to be. Then, at other times, I have the feeling that this is all part of a scheme and she has set her cap at me."

"That is indeed a pickle. I know you would have no compunction about putting a schemer in her place, but if Miss"—Anne looked over at the maid who was there to play propriety—"that is, if the young woman is indeed an innocent, I know you would not wish to be unkind."

"Precisely." He had known that Anne would understand his dilemma.

"Still, there are only a few days left. Then she will leave, and with luck you will not have to meet her until after she is safely wed. But tell me, is there no other woman present who catches your fancy? Surely she would leave you in peace, were you to begin courting another."

The only woman he wanted was in this room. But mindful of their audience he did not press his suit. He had promised Anne he would give her time to consider his proposal, and that was what he would do.

"The young ladies have all formed attachments, or so it seems," he said at last. "Not that I have much time to notice. I have my hands full avoiding the girl while at the same time keeping my eyes on Priscilla. I swear Priscilla is more trouble than the rest of my sisters put together."

"I am certain it is just youthful high spirits. And she must be looking forward to her ball."

The summer Elizabeth had turned eighteen, Lady Frederick had arranged a house party and ball to celebrate her daughter's birthday. The custom had continued for each of his sisters, and each occasion had been grander than the last. Priscilla's would be the finest yet, with a special treat that he had arranged for her from London.

Freddie was genuinely fond of his sister, and he had looked forward to seeing her enjoying the celebrations. But the presence of Miss Sommersby had tainted the occasion for him.

"Indeed. It is all she talks about. In one moment she is sure she will be a triumph and the next she worries that foul weather will keep away most of the guests."

Besides their house guests, Priscilla and his mother had invited every person of rank who lived within an easy drive.

Anne gave a wistful smile. "I am certain it will be a splendid occasion, and that Priscilla will be the envy of every other young lady present. I only wish I could see it for myself."

It struck him that Anne had probably not been to a ball since her own first Season in London,

seven long years ago. This, too, she had given up.
He felt a sudden urge to make up to her for all
the things that she had missed out on in those
years. "But of course you shall be there. You will
be my guest."

He heard a dull thud and turned to see the maid,
having knocked her sewing basket onto the floor,
was staring at him gape-mouthed. "Beg your pardon," the maid said, as she bent down and began
gathering up the contents that had spilled.

"I do not think that would be wise," Anne said.

"Why not?"

Bright spots of anger flared in Anne's cheeks.
"You know the gossip. Do you want everyone saying
that you brought your mistress to your sister's ball?"
she demanded, seeming to forget that they had an
audience.

"We both know that is not true."

"The truth does not matter. What matters is what
people think. Your mother would have an apoplexy
at the sight of me. Half your guests would give me
the cut direct, while the other—"

"Stop." He could not bear to hear her disparage
herself. "Let us make a bargain, you and I. If my
mother sends you an invitation, you will agree to
come. As her guest, there can be no question of any
impropriety."

"I would wager a hundred pounds that Lady
Frederick would cut off her own hand rather than
write that invitation."

"Then there is no reason for you not to agree, is
there?"

After a moment of thought, Anne nodded. "I
agree. But I think you are being foolish."

"You just leave this to me."

It was a stupid wager. He knew that, and yet he had invited her to the ball out of friendship. Still, there had to be a way to convince his mother to invite Anne. After all, the ball was only one evening. What would his mother think if she knew he had invited Anne to become his wife?

As he rode back home, he considered how he would best approach his mother. Should he request that she invite Anne as a favor to him? No, it was unlikely she would agree. Perhaps he should enlist Elizabeth, gain her support first. But no, there was no need to drag Elizabeth into the middle of this. He would simply go to his mother and not allow her to intimidate him. He would not argue or plead, but instead be firm until his mother gave in.

As he was entering the house, a footman informed him that Lady Frederick wished to see her son at once. He tried to see this as an opportunity, but his heart was heavy, for he knew there was little chance that he could live up to the bargain he had made with Anne.

Pausing outside the door to his mother's sitting room, he squared his shoulders. *I will be calm,* he reminded himself. *Even if she says no today, it is not the end of the world. There are still several days before the ball to convince her to change her mind.*

He knocked on the door.

"Enter," she called.

Freddie opened the door and was surprised to see his mother was not seated in her favorite chair, but instead had apparently been pacing the room. "You wished to see me?"

"Yes," the Dowager Lady Frederick said.

He closed the door behind him, and felt the familiar sense of suffocation. Of all the rooms in the house, this was the one he liked least. His mother had chosen to decorate it in the style of her youth. In one corner stood a French writing desk, while in the other was the sofa upon which Lady Frederick preferred to recline while reading. Scattered throughout the room were upholstered chairs that appeared too fragile to bear his weight, next to small lace-covered tables displaying ceramic figurines and other objets d'art. One could hardly move for fear of bumping into something.

He waited for his mother to speak, but instead she crossed to the window, placing one hand on the lace curtain as she looked out over the estate. From her situation she could see the gardens and the park that led down to the lake. But from her expression he knew that she was not seeing the beauty of the estate; something else was preying on her mind.

Then she turned to him and spoke.

"I have seen the child," she said.

"The child?"

She released the curtain and turned to face him. "Anne Webster's brat. I was out driving when I passed by the old manor, and there he was."

"You mean you went there to spy on Anne," he said angrily, appalled that she would stoop so low. The Websters' residence lay to the east, while the village of New Biddeford lay to the west. There was no reason for her to have driven by Anne's unless she had done so deliberately.

"I went there to see for myself. And now that I

have, I have one question for you. You have never lied to me before, so I expect the truth now. Is that boy your son?"

He felt as if the wind had been knocked out of him. "My son? How could you think such a thing? Do you have so little regard for me as to believe I would father a bastard child and not accept responsibility for what I had done? What kind of man do you think I am?" His disbelief turned to anger. How dare she accuse him of this?

His mother seemed to sag with relief. "Then he is not your son."

"No. But would to God he were." If only Ian had been his child and Anne's. Then there would have been every reason for her to marry him. Instead, out of concern for Ian, there was a strong possibility that Anne would refuse his offer.

"How can you say such a thing? Have you lost all sense of propriety?"

"Because it is true. Any man would be proud to claim Ian as his son."

His mother shook her head. "I swear to you, I do not know you anymore. Ever since that trollop Anne Webster—"

"Enough," he said, in a voice that was not quite a shout. "Anne Webster has done nothing that deserves your condemnation. You will speak of her respectfully or not at all."

Lady Frederick glared at him. "You were always quick to defend her. But what would you think if Priscilla had behaved in that way?"

"I pray to God Priscilla is never put to the test. But if she were, I would hope that she would behave with the same sense of duty and courage Anne has shown."

"Duty? Courage? You have completely lost your wits. If only your father were here to see this."

For once the admonition brought no sense of shame or failure. He would not let his mother cow him by reminding him of how much he had to live up to.

"But Father is not here. And as you constantly remind me, *I* am Viscount Frederick. If you do not approve of how I choose to live my life, then you may feel free to depart. You can have your choice of properties, so long as you are out from under my roof."

There was a hiss of indrawn breath. His mother appeared shocked. He had never argued with her before, let alone threatened to banish her. But never before had the stakes been this high. He would not—could not—let his mother rule his life. He had to make her understand this, or he would never be free to be his own man.

"You would not dare."

"Try me."

"But what about Priscilla?"

"Priscilla may stay or go as she pleases. She will always be welcome here."

The silence stretched on between them. He could not believe that his mother was actually considering his threat. He had expected her to capitulate rather than give up her position as the Lady of Beechwood Park.

Finally she said, "I will stay, and I will hold my tongue. But you can not rule my thoughts. And when you find yourself disgraced, you can expect no sympathy from me. I only hope I can protect Priscilla from the consequences of her brother's folly."

It hurt to realize that his own mother had so little faith in his character or his judgment. All these years of trying to live up to her impossibly high standards had been for naught. He could never please her.

"Understood," he said grimly. "And there is one more thing. Tomorrow morning you will send Anne Webster an invitation to the ball."

"I will not."

"You will, or I assure you, dear Mother, I will not be in attendance." He would have threatened to cancel the ball altogether, but that would not have been fair to Priscilla.

"But what will our guests say?"

"Our guests will take their cue from you. If you tell them Anne is an old friend of the family, then they will accept her."

"There will be talk—"

"I expect you to see that there is none. I expect Anne to be treated as an honored guest. If I see otherwise, then I warn you, our bargain is off."

"Do you love her?" His mother said the word "love" as if it were a contagion to be feared.

"I do not know," he answered honestly. He felt a closeness to Anne that he had never felt with another. He enjoyed her friendship, and he strongly wanted to care for her and to save her from her current situation. But would his feelings for her have been so strong if she did not need his care? Was he simply playing protector, as he had when they were children?

And was there any hope that she loved him, as

something more than a friend and the brother she had never had?

His mother seemed to take some comfort in his admission. "At least you are not totally lost to reason. I will send Anne Webster an invitation. Perhaps this is all for the best, for once you have a chance to see her mixing with ladies of quality, you will be able to form a true judgment of her character and worth."

"As you say." He did not need to see Anne in a public role to know her worth. But perhaps, once she had seen Anne, his mother might soften her opinion toward her.

If not, then this first confrontation with his mother would not be the last. One way or another, he meant to have Anne for his wife. If Lady Frederick was unable to accept this, she would have to take up residence elsewhere. Anne had suffered enough. He would not allow his mother or anyone else to hurt her.

Ten

Anne looked down at the stiff vellum card in her hand. On it, in copperplate script was written, "The Viscountess Frederick requests the pleasure of your company at a ball to celebrate the birthday of her daughter, Miss Priscilla Pennington." Anne turned the card over, certain that it was a mistake. But no, there was her name, written on the other side in the same elegant hand.

"I do not understand," she said at last.

"I assure you, it is no mistake," Mrs. Elizabeth Rutledge replied.

Anne could not believe this was happening. It was only yesterday that Freddie had recklessly invited her to his sister's ball. Anne would have wagered any amount that no such invitation would be forthcoming. Yet here it was, delivered in person by his own sister.

She should never have made that foolish bargain with Freddie. She had thought herself long past such impulsive behavior. Yet when Freddie had challenged her, she had reacted as if they were still children, recklessly agreeing to his bargain without pausing to consider what it would mean if he won.

"But why would she invite me?"

"I can not say," Elizabeth replied. "But I assure you the invitation is genuine, and when you attend you will find my mother is anxious to show you every courtesy and respect."

Anne smiled bitterly. If Lady Frederick wanted to show Anne every courtesy, then she would have called upon her. Or invited Anne to visit her at Beechwood Park. No, she saw the fine hand of Freddie behind this invitation. Yet how on earth had he convinced his mother to invite her? She had not credited him with such powers of persuasion.

Anne smiled wryly. "I doubt very much that Lady Frederick would truly be pleased to see me. However, it is of no consequence. It would not be proper for me to attend. Other considerations notwithstanding, I am still in mourning for my father."

She was surprised at how disappointed she felt. She had no wish to expose herself to the censure of her neighbors. But there was a small, girlish part of her that wished just once she could go to a ball and give herself over to her own enjoyment. She could not remember the last time she had been free to consider only her own wishes. Ever since Ian's birth, she had been forced to set aside her own wants to care for him. She loved him, and knew that whatever sacrifices she made for his sake were amply repaid by his love for her. But at times, like this one, she could not help wishing that just for one night she could put her cares aside.

Mrs. Rutledge waved one hand dismissively. "It has been three months since his death. And this is not

London, but a country ball, held for a girl you have known since she was born. No one will think it remarkable if you attend."

"But I have nothing to wear," she said, surprised to find that a part of herself was actually considering the idea.

Elizabeth looked her over critically. "We are much of a size, I think. If you permit me, I would be pleased to send over one of my gowns. It is no trouble, for I have far more than I can possibly wear. Your maid can make any alterations necessary."

"I can not accept."

"But you must. I insist."

"Why are you doing this?" It was not as if Elizabeth Rutledge had been a close friend of hers. And for all Elizabeth knew, Anne was indeed a sinner, the mother of a bastard child. Yet Elizabeth was showing her far more kindness than Anne had any right to expect.

Elizabeth looked at Anne, and then glanced down at her hands in apparent fascination. After a moment she looked up and began to speak. "It was a very difficult time for me when Lieutenant Carson, my first husband, died. Our daughter was scarce a week old when he was killed in battle. When Freddie heard the news, he did not send a mere letter of condolence, but came all the way to Portugal. He settled John's affairs, and then, when I was strong enough, brought Mary and me back to England. I don't know what I would have done without him."

"Your brother is a good man," Anne said, wondering why Elizabeth had chosen this moment to share her story. Anne needed no one to tell her of Freddie's kindness.

Mrs. Rutledge took a deep breath. "Eventually, as the first shock wore off, I realized that my husband had left us virtually penniless. He would have provided for us, I am sure. But he did not expect to die so soon, and in the end we were left with nothing. Freddie settled a generous allowance on me, and made the provisions for Mary that her father should have. Many a brother would have been reluctant to assume such a burden, would have wished me to find another husband. After my time of mourning, I had several respectable offers. I would have accepted one of them, but Freddie said no. He told me there was no reason to marry, except for love."

Anne swallowed against a lump in her throat. She knew too well what it felt like to be a woman alone, with no husband or protector. Elizabeth had been fortunate indeed to have a brother who cared so much for her.

"But why are you telling me this?"

"I have had more than my share of happiness. I have found love, not once but twice. All I have ever wished for my brother is that he find the same kind of happiness for himself. And I know in my heart that Miss Sommersby is not the kind of woman who will make him happy."

Anne felt her own heart stir. "And you think I will make him happy?"

"I do not know if he loves you, or if you love him. But he deserves a chance to find out. I would rather see him happy with a woman of your reputation than see him married to a paragon and miserable."

A woman of her reputation. Anne winced, even as she admired his sister for her plain speaking.

"I will think about it," she said at last.

"Do not think about it. Just say you will come," Mrs. Rutledge said firmly. "In a few weeks you will return to Canada. This might be your only chance. I do not want my brother to spend another seven years waiting for you to return."

Anne felt herself coloring. "You must be mistaken," she said. "Freddie has proposed marriage to several women over the years. Surely that shows he was not pining for any one lady in particular."

"So I thought as well," her visitor said. "But now I see it differently. Strange, is it not, that he should pay his addresses only to those women who were likely to reject him?"

"It is a coincidence," Anne insisted.

"It may be. And it may not. But the next step is up to you. Will you come to the ball?"

"Yes," Anne said, suddenly anxious to find out if there was any truth to Mrs. Rutledge's assertion. Had Freddie, perhaps without even realizing it, been waiting for her? It could not be. They had shared friendship and a childhood romance. Nothing more. His offer to marry her had been prompted by compassion rather than love. And yet, was there a chance that there could be something more between them? She owed it to them both to find out.

Mrs. Rutledge wasted no time. That very afternoon, she sent over her own maid, and not one but three gowns for Anne to choose from. Anne led the maid up to her bedroom, then watched anxiously as the maid began to unpack the dresses.

The first was of dove gray silk, with long full sleeves, trimmed in lace. The neckline was high and modest, and would have done credit to a bishop's wife.

Anne allowed the maid to help her into the gown, then examined her reflection in the pier. "A governess," she said.

"Miss?"

"Never mind," Anne said. On second thought, she looked less like a governess and more like a penitent sinner. "Let us try the next one."

The second gown was of sheer lace layered over white satin, trimmed with white and scarlet ribbons. "I can change the ribbons, if you like," the maid offered.

"It is not the ribbons that are the problem," Anne said. The satin underdress clung to every curve of her body, leaving nothing to the imagination. Her shoulders were completely uncovered, and the neckline was so low that she feared disaster.

The maid tugged the neckline, adjusting the silk ribbon that gathered the bodice. "This is very stylish, miss. I just need to let it out a bit, on top. And take in the waist."

There was not enough fabric in the world to make this dress decent. Anne did not care what they were wearing in London these days. She felt half-naked, and while it might be amusing to see Freddie's reaction, she could not face down a room of strangers wearing this dress.

"I am certain your mistress is quite à la mode. But I am used to a simpler style," Anne said.

The maid sniffed disdainfully, but unwrapped the third gown.

It took one glimpse, and Anne fell in love. The gown was a deep violet silk, with long fitted sleeves, and a double row of scalloped flounces. The neckline was square, lower than had been fashionable when Anne made her debut, but not so low as to be immodest.

Anne sighed happily as the maid helped her into the gown and began to fasten the delicate buttons in the back.

"This is beautiful," she said with delight, as she slowly turned and admired her reflection. She could not remember the last time she had worn such a garment, one which made her feel every inch an elegant lady.

The maid permitted herself a smile. "The mistress thought as how this was the one you would fancy. She had it made up this season, but then decided the color didn't suit her."

Reaching into her sewing box, the maid withdrew a packet of pins. "Now just stay still while I mark where we need to take this in," she said.

Anne stood still, then turned slowly as the maid marked the waist and pinned up the hem.

"Lucky for you that you and the mistress are close enough in size to be sisters," the maid observed, as she helped Anne out of the gown. "It won't take me more than a couple of hours to take this in for you."

"There is no need for you to do it. I can see to it, or one of my maids will," Anne protested.

"No." The maid shook her head firmly. "Mrs. Rutledge told me I was to do this myself, and that's what I mean to do. I'm not letting some half-trained country maid ruin a London gown."

"Very well," Anne said, secretly relieved. Her own sewing was good enough for Ian's sturdy clothing, but a cambric shirt was hardly a silk ball gown. And her maids were as like to ruin the dress as not, out of sheer inexperience.

The day of the ball arrived. It was just twilight as Anne's carriage approached Beechwood Park. From a distance she could see that the house was ablaze with lights. Light streamed from the open great doors and from every window. Torches illuminated the grand staircase leading up to the hall, while in the east garden paper lanterns lined the paths.

As her carriage turned onto the drive, Anne's pulse began to race and her breath quickened. She could not do this. It would be a repeat of the scene in the lending library, only a thousand times worse. She fought a craven urge to tell her coachmen to turn around and return her home.

But one thought sustained her. She could still hear Elizabeth Rutledge's voice: *I do not know if he loves you, or if you love him. But he deserves a chance to find out.*

It was what she hoped for, and at the same time dreaded. If he loved her, would it be enough? Could they make a life together for themselves and for Ian? Or, in the end, would they have to part, as much for Freddie's sake as for her own?

In the end, her innate stubbornness came to her rescue. She had nothing to be ashamed of. She owed it to herself, and to Freddie, to see if there was a chance that she could be accepted back into polite society.

The carriage drew to a halt as she finished her musings. A footman opened the door and helped her to step out. Anne lifted her chin and squared her shoulders, steeling herself for whatever would come.

Once in the entranceway, she handed her cloak to a footman, then made her way to the ballroom. Just inside the door, Freddie, Lady Frederick and Miss Priscilla stood greeting their guests. As she approached she saw them greeting Sir William and Lady Dunne.

Her heart sank into her stomach as she approached the gauntlet, realizing she was about to be put to the test. For all Anne knew, the invitation was but a ploy, part of Lady Frederick's plan to humiliate her publicly and thus ensure that Frederick was forced to cut his connection to her.

And then Freddie saw her, and he smiled. When his eyes caught hers, she could see that he was truly pleased that she had come. Anne felt herself smiling in return.

The Dunnes moved away, and she found herself face to face with her adversary, Lady Frederick.

"Good evening, Lord Frederick, Lady Frederick," she said, with a carefully measured curtesy. "It was so kind of you to invite me."

There was a brief moment of silence, and then Freddie gently nudged his mother. "Miss Webster," the dowager said, inclining her head in acknowledgment.

"We are pleased that you could join us," Freddie said. His gaze left her face for the first time, and his smile broadened in appreciation as he took in her elegant appearance. Then he turned to his sister. "And of course you remember my sister, Priscilla?"

When Anne had last seen Priscilla, she had been a child in the schoolroom. Now she was a beautiful young woman, who was bound to be breaking hearts in London. "Miss Priscilla. May I present my felicitations on your birthday? And my hope that you find much happiness in the coming year."

Priscilla extended her hand for Anne to grasp. "Miss Webster. I am so pleased you could be here. I look forward to improving our acquaintance," she said, with a mischievous glance at her mother.

Lady Frederick turned a shade paler, but did not reprove her daughter's levity.

Anne turned her head and saw that there were easily two dozen guests in the salon. Her palms felt damp as she realized that Lady Frederick was just the first test of the evening. Now she had to endure a room full of near strangers. And Freddie, consumed with his duties as host, would not be there to protect her.

But she needn't have worried. Just as she gathered her courage, she saw Mrs. Rutledge making her way toward them.

As he caught sight of his sister Freddie muttered, "At last."

"Miss Webster. How pleasant to see you this evening," Mrs. Rutledge said.

"I am happy to be here," Anne said. "And I must thank you again for the loan of this beautiful gown."

Lady Frederick shot her daughter a fierce look,

and Anne realized that she had not known about
the gown.

"Do not mention it," Mrs. Rutledge said. Turning
to her brother, she added, "The refreshments have
been set out in the Chinese salon, and I have told
the musicians that we will begin in half an hour."

"Thank you," he said.

"And now, Miss Webster, permit me to take you
around and introduce you to our guests. You will
know some of them, of course, but there are many
here who are eager to make your acquaintance." So
saying, Mrs. Rutledge linked her arm in Anne's and
led her away.

Anne experienced a flash of humor as she realized
how thoroughly she was being managed.

Just beyond the receiving line was the blue salon,
where card tables had been set up. But this early in
the evening, the guests had gathered to talk. As they
entered the room, Mrs. Rutledge's eyes scanned the
assembled company. "I know this is difficult for you,
but you must pretend to be at your ease. And whatever anyone says, do not take offense. Simply give
them your haughtiest stare and pretend that they
have not spoken. Can you do that?"

"Yes."

Mrs. Rutledge led her over to a group consisting
of Sir William and Lady Dunne, Mr. and Mrs. Bennett and the widowed Mrs. Price. They were con-
temporaries of her parents, neighbors she had
known all her life. It was from them that she could
expect the harshest criticisms.

As she drew near she could hear Sir William saying,
"So then he married her!" There was polite laughter,
which trailed off as they caught sight of Anne.

"Good evening," Mrs. Rutledge said. "I believe you all remember Anne Webster? She has recently returned to the neighborhood, and we are so pleased she could join us this evening."

Anne found herself the focus of five pairs of eyes.

Mrs. Price fixed Anne with a weak watery gaze. "How do you do?" she said. Her memory had been failing for years, and it was clear she did not remember who Anne was.

Mr. Bennett gave Anne a cold stare. "Miss Webster. My condolences on the loss of your father. He was a good neighbor and a true gentleman. He will be greatly missed."

"Thank you," Anne said.

"We had heard you had returned. And it was said there was a son . . ." Mrs. Bennett's voice trailed off.

"Adopted son," Mrs. Rutledge said firmly. "And it shows great charity for Miss Webster to have taken on such a responsibility."

Anne hid a start of surprise. Adopted son? It was the truth, but how had Mrs. Rutledge known? Had Freddie told her? Or had she concocted the explanation on her own?

"But I thought—" Lady Dunne said, then was interrupted by her husband.

"Humph. Adopted son. Very Christian of you," Sir William said. He was a bluff man, who hid a good heart under his gruff nature. She could see him casting about for an unexceptionable topic. "Have you decided what you will do about the Manor?"

"Not yet," Anne said.

The others took up the new topic.

"If you are of a mind to sell the property, I would be willing to make you a fair offer," Mr. Bennett said.

"Whatever you do, don't rent the property to strangers. You never know what sort of people might want to rent a country house. Why, my cousin allowed her agent to rent her manor house, only to find that he had rented it out to a Cit and his family. They were the most dreadful toad-eating mushrooms, who tried to bull their way into society. My cousin's neighbors still have not forgiven her," Lady Dunne said.

"I will remember that," Anne said, stifling the urge to laugh at the absurdity of it all. Prior to this evening, she would have wagered that the good souls of New Biddeford would have preferred anyone, even the most vulgar of Cits, to her own presence in the neighborhood.

They chatted briefly for a moment more, and then Mrs. Rutledge made their excuses. She continued around the blue salon before guiding Anne into the ballroom and reacquainting her with her former neighbors and introducing her to some of Priscilla's guests from London. She met the sisters Crane, and Lady Alice, but waited in vain for an introduction to Freddie's nemesis, Miss Sommersby.

Anne's trepidation was beginning to fade. No one mentioned Ian or made any reference to the rumors that had circulated. It seemed that the guests were prepared to accept her as Anne Webster, daughter of country gentry, rather than Anne Webster, notorious sinner. She felt only a brief moment of unease when Mrs. Rutledge left to supervise last-minute preparations, but soon found herself chatting with a group of young ladies. It was surprisingly easy. All she had to do was ask about their experiences in London, then smile and nod as they prattled on.

From the corner of her eye she saw a stir in the crowd, and she turned to see Freddie leading his sister into the ballroom.

"Doesn't she look divine? It's such a shame her brother is so ordinary," one of the ladies said.

"He may be ordinary looking, but he is a viscount," said another.

The ladies giggled in unison.

"I think Lord Frederick is handsome," Anne said fiercely. "And there is more to measuring a man than his title."

Her companions stared at her in incomprehension. But any remark they would have made was cut off by the arrival of the gentlemen who had come to claim their partners for the first dance.

Anne had not planned on dancing this evening. It was enough simply to be here and to watch the others. She accepted a glass of champagne from a passing footman, then joined in conversation with another woman who had chosen to sit out the first dance. But she found her attention was not on what the woman was saying; rather, it was on Freddie as he led his sister to the top of the set.

She could not understand why the girl had referred to Freddie as ordinary. True he was of only average height, but his figure was good, and from one look at his features you could tell that he was a kind person. Indeed, there was nothing to fault in his appearance. He had eschewed the excesses of the dandy set, and favored the simple elegance of a midnight blue coat with dark trousers and a shirt of brilliant white.

The musicians struck up the tune, and Freddie, smiling down upon his sister, took her hand and led her in the first steps of the dance. Seeing them together, Anne wished suddenly that it was she and not Priscilla whose hand lay in his and that it was she who was the object of his smiles.

Eleven

After leading Priscilla out to start the ball, Freddie then partnered Lady Alice Westmoreland, who as a duke's daughter was the highest ranking of his female guests. He then danced with the oldest Miss Crane, followed by her younger sister, before he danced with the unfortunate Miss Flockhart, whose height made it difficult for her to find partners. Most gentlemen did not wish a dance partner who looked down upon them.

He danced and talked and acted mechanically. Yet a moment later he could not remember what he had said or what the dance had been. All of his attention was fixed on Anne.

He wished that he could go to her, but did not want to create more gossip by showing any undue partiality. Not when they had worked so hard to scotch the rumors. He did not know what story his mother had spread, but whatever she and Elizabeth had concocted was doing the trick.

Or it could be that the arrivals from London had brought with them fresh scandals that were of more interest than old news. The latest *on-dit* was that a certain duchess had been discovered in bed with her son-in-law, and his guests, while professing themselves shocked, could talk of little else.

Whatever the reason, Anne was enjoying herself. His senses were in tune with her so that he could read her enjoyment in the tilt of her head and in the sparkle of her eyes.

He wondered why she was not dancing. He knew she had had offers—he had seen to it himself. But instead she stayed on the sidelines, apparently content to watch the gaiety. At least she was not alone. She was often in conversation with other ladies, and more than one gentleman chose to sit out a set with her.

He felt himself pulled in two directions. A part of him was the Viscount Frederick. This was the part that was the conscientious host, watching over his guests and ensuring that everything went smoothly.

And there was a part of him that he thought of as Freddie. That part knew at every instant precisely where Anne was and what she was doing. That part longed to spend the evening with her, be damned to what propriety said.

After the set he escorted Miss Flockhart to the sidelines. He saw his mother conversing with the Sommersbys. He tried not to let her catch his eye, but his mother signaled, and he realized he could not ignore her.

Reluctantly he went over to where she stood. "Yes, Mother. You wished for something?"

"The Sommersbys were just complimenting me on the musicians. They came from London, did they not?"

He gave his mother a sharp look, certain that she was up to something.

"Yes, we hired them from London. Mr. Sotheby is their leader, I believe," he said. A fact which his mother knew only too well, as she had made the arrangements for this evening. Freddie's sole contribution had been the special entertainment planned for later on.

"Good evening, Lord Frederick," Miss Sommersby said, as she joined their circle. "I must compliment you on a splendid entertainment."

"Thank you," he replied.

The musicians struck up a waltz. He waited a moment and then realized that no partner was coming to claim Miss Sommersby.

"George," his mother said, using the name that he hated. "I am certain Miss Sommersby would be honored to partner you for this dance."

He shook his head firmly. "Alas, but I am promised to another," he lied. "If you will excuse me?"

As he crossed the room he could feel his mother's gaze boring holes in his back. But he would not let her maneuver him into showing Miss Sommersby any particular attention.

In a moment he reached the alcove where Anne was standing in conversation with Elizabeth and her husband, David. "Miss Webster, I believe you promised me a waltz, and I am here to collect on your promise."

She hesitated. "I did not come to dance," she said at last.

"Nonsense. It is a ball after all. And you can hardly refuse your host."

With that, he took her hand in his and, in a mood that would brook no resistance, led her onto the dance floor.

"I warn you, I am sadly out of practice. I take no responsibility for any injury you may suffer," Anne said.

He placed his arms around her. "I am willing to suffer the consequences," he said.

The musicians struck up a waltz, and they began to dance.

He could not have planned this better. No country dance, but the oh-so-slightly-scandalous waltz, that gave a gentleman the excuse to put his arms around a lady and to partner only her for the duration of the dance.

He could not help smiling. For the first time this evening he was actually enjoying himself.

Anne's face bore a look of intense concentration for the first measures, as she concentrated on her steps. But then she relaxed as her feet remembered them, and she gave herself over to the rhythm of the music.

At last she raised her eyes to his face. "Poor Freddie," she said. "I take it you used me as an excuse to avoid Miss Sommersby?"

"No," he said. "Well, yes actually, but it wasn't the way it sounds."

"Do not worry, I will not take offense. I am happy to oblige you."

He looked into her eyes, willing her to believe him. "You should give yourself more credit. I could have asked any woman to dance. But I have been waiting to dance with you all evening."

It was the simple truth. He had been stunned by her appearance. He had grown used to her being in the dull grays and blacks of mourning, seeing her still as his childhood friend. The violet silk gown had not so much transformed her as it had reminded him that she was a beautiful and desirable woman. No wonder the rumors had circulated concerning his attentions to her. Seeing her outer beauty, who would believe that a man felt no more than friendship for her?

"I take it you approve of my appearance? You do not think the gown is too young for me?" He heard the uncertainty in her voice.

"You look beautiful," he assured her. "Even now, Miss Sommersby and her friends are gnashing their teeth with envy."

She laughed. "If only it were true."

But it was. Miss Sommersby was still a girl, on the verge of womanhood. She was lovely, but unfinished. Anne had the grace and beauty of a woman. Her face was yet unlined, but in it one could read the strength of her character. Seeing the two women tonight made it clear how different they were, how much Miss Sommersby suffered in comparison with her rival. He could only marvel that he had not seen this before.

"Are you enjoying yourself?" he asked, conscious that he had been admiring her for far too long.

"Yes. I must admit that you were right. I am grateful that you convinced me to attend. I only hope my newly repaired reputation can survive the sight of us waltzing." She frowned as she looked around the room, but with the exception of his mother, no one seemed to be paying them any particular attention.

He felt a pang of nervousness. He had not meant to risk her reputation, but he would not have given up this waltz for the world. "If anyone asks, say that

I simply collected an old debt. Remember, you had promised me your first waltz in London."

Seven years ago, Anne had been nervous at the prospect of her first London Season. Her mother had died the year before, and her sister was married and living with her husband in Canada. She had only a distant cousin to advise her, someone Anne had never met before. Sensing Anne's unease, Freddie had tried to cheer her up by promising to claim her first dance.

But he had never seen Anne during her Season. News of Lieutenant Carson's death had reached him soon after his arrival in London, and Freddie had left the country to bring his sister home. There was nothing else he could have done. But now he could not help wondering how much different their lives would have been if he had had a chance to court Anne properly. Would they have fallen in love, or would they have remained mere friends? Perhaps it had taken losing her and then finding her after all these years to make him realize what he had lost?

The music came to an end. Around them gentlemen bowed to their partners and ladies curtseyed, but he did not release Anne. He was not ready to let her go.

She seemed to sense the conflict inside him. She squeezed his hand in hers and then stepped back, forcing him to drop his arms.

The orchestra leader tapped his baton on the music stand, signaling for attention.

"Wait," Freddie said, realizing what was to come next.

"Ladies and gentlemen, in honor of Miss Priscilla Pennington's birthday, her brother, Viscount

Frederick, has arranged a special entertainment for the guests. Those who wish to view it should proceed through these doors onto the south lawn."

The announcement brought a hum of conversation and a shriek of delight from Priscilla. The minx must have guessed what he had planned for her. He had kept the secret as best he could, but he had run out of explanations for the sudden increase in the groundskeeping staff or ways to describe just what it was they were doing on the south lawn.

He linked Anne's arm through his. "Come with me," he said. "You will enjoy this."

He and Anne joined the stream of guests who were eager to see this promised entertainment. Passing through the French doors, they descended the marble staircase onto the lawn, which was bordered on either side by shrubbery. Chinese lanterns had been placed about on the shrubbery and on poles set into the lawn. The lanterns had the curious effect of illuminating the central space, but served to cast the areas on the side into even deeper shadows.

At the bottom of the steps, he drew her off to the side of the terrace. His guests streamed past him, following the lantern-lit paths to the open space before them.

"What is this?" she asked.

"Be patient." He smiled. He had intended this as a treat for Priscilla, but it would give him even more pleasure to share this with Anne.

He watched as the guests assembled. Some of the ladies had paused to put on their shawls, but the night was so warm that they were not really needed. Chairs had been placed in a semicircle on the lawn, and a few of the older guests, his mother among them, claimed the seats for their own.

A man materialized from the shadows. "Everything is ready. Just give the word."

Freddie looked around. There was no one coming down the steps, and the last of the stragglers had found places for themselves. He saw Priscilla in the center of the crowd, flanked by Elizabeth and David.

Freddie nodded. "You may begin."

The man, who looked like a groundskeeper, disappeared back into the shadows.

A few moments later, there was a loud crack as if of cannon shot, and then a red star blossomed high above them in the sky.

The crowd gasped in delight.

Anne's face was turned up to the sky, her eyes shining and her mouth open wide with delight. "Fireworks! How lovely."

They were pretty, he supposed, but he found it more enjoyable to watch Anne's reaction.

There was another boom, and a yellow flower appeared, followed by a white star and then a red fountain that threw off long streamers that nearly reached to the ground. As each rocket was set off, the explosion vibrated the very ground, while the fireworks painted the sky in fantastic patterns.

"What a marvelous present for your sister," Anne said, still not taking her eyes from the spectacle.

"It was nothing," he said. "Priscilla has been begging me for the last year to take her to Vauxhall Gardens, to see the illuminations. But Vauxhall is not the safest of places for an impressionable girl. So instead I brought the fireworks to her." It had cost a small fortune to persuade the illuminators to leave London and put on this display. But it would make Priscilla happy and would ensure that her ball was the most talked-about event of the summer.

"You are the best of brothers," Anne said.

The word "brother" scraped against his nerve endings. He did not want her to admire him for his kindness. He did not want her to see him as simply a good brother. He did not even want to be her friend.

"Come," he said, taking her by the arm. He pulled her away from the steps, into the shrubbery where the shadows were thickest.

Letting go of her arm, he turned to face her. He cupped her face between his hands. Time seemed to stop for a moment, and then he bent his head down and his lips brushed hers. Her lips were soft and warm beneath his. He drew his head back for a moment, saw the surprise in her eyes and the flush in her cheeks.

He dropped his hands down and took her hands in his. He raised them to his lips, kissing first the left and then the right. He then placed her hands on his shoulders and drew her into his embrace.

His heart was racing as he bent his lips down to hers again. This time she returned his kiss, eagerly pressing her lips against his own. He opened his mouth and let his tongue trace the outline of her mouth. She parted her lips, and his tongue passed inside, tasting her sweetness.

Every nerve of his body tingled. He tightened his embrace, rejoicing in the feel of her softness as her body was pressed against his. As he lifted his head from hers, he realized her breathing was as ragged as his own. He brushed his lips against hers, then continued down, kissing her jaw and her neck, the soft hollow of her throat, and he felt the pounding of her pulse.

He knew this was madness. He should stop at once. They were sure to be discovered. And he would stop. Just one more kiss, he promised himself. And then another . . .

From a distance he heard the sounds of applause. The part of him that was Viscount Frederick, realized the fireworks must have come to an end, and without that distraction, he and Anne were now in grave danger of being discovered.

"Freddie." Anne breathed out his name.

Reluctantly his hands ceased their exploration. He drew her to him in a fierce embrace and then, reluctantly, stepped back and let her go. "We will talk. Tomorrow."

"Yes." She tugged the shoulders of her gown into place.

"I am afraid that is not enough," he said. "You have the look of a woman who has been thoroughly kissed."

Indeed her lips were swollen, and her face was flushed with the beginnings of desire. It was all he could do not to take her in his arms and kiss her again.

And as for himself, his skintight breeches left no doubt as to the depths of the passion she had aroused in him.

"You go in first, then I will follow in a moment," Anne said.

He shook his head. "No," he said. "Come with me, and we will go in by the side door." With luck they could avoid those who were no doubt looking for him, to congratulate him on the brilliant spectacle he had provided.

But even if they were seen together, by tomorrow it would not matter. After tonight, he had no doubt that Anne felt the same passion for him that he felt for her. He would propose again for form's sake, but this time he was certain her answer would be yes.

Twelve

The day after the ball, Anne could not remember how she had returned home or whom she had spoken with after she had parted from Freddie. When he had kissed her, the relationship between them had changed forever. His touch had awakened feelings in her that she had never known. And, to be honest, it had not been just that he had kissed her. She had returned his kisses, matching his enthusiasm with her own. For the first time in her life, she had felt what it was to desire a man and to be desired in return.

It was wonderful. It was glorious. It was a disaster. She knew that when Freddie called on her, he would expect her to agree to marry him. She blushed as she remembered that she had given him little reason to doubt her feelings.

Yet there was more than their own happiness to consider. There was Ian's future as well. Last night, the guests had seemed prepared to accept Anne into their society. But how long would their acceptance last? Would it extend to young Ian? Or was she letting her newly discovered passion overwhelm her common sense?

Just then there was a knock on the door to her
sitting room. "Enter," she called.

The door opened, revealing the butler Mr. Boswell.
"A Captain Montgomery wishes an audience with
you," he said.

She searched her mind, but could not remember
if there had been a Captain Montgomery among the
guests at last night's ball. "Did he say anything else?"

"He said the nature of his errand was confidential," Mr. Boswell said with a disapproving sniff.
Clearly he felt the stranger's reluctance to confide
in him was a slur upon his integrity.

"I will meet him in the library," Anne decided.

Descending the stairs, she puzzled over the identity of her caller. Perhaps he was here because of
some business with her father.

As she entered the library, she saw a man standing
in front of the fireplace, his attention fixed on the
portrait of her mother. He wore the dress coat of a
naval captain, and his close-cropped hair was the
most brilliant shade of red that she had ever seen.

"Good morning," she said.

The captain turned, and she realized that she did
not know him, although his appearance was vaguely
familiar. "A remarkable likeness," he said. "I had
almost forgotten how beautiful Sarah was."

His words struck a chill in her heart. It was not
what he said, but the tone of his voice. He sounded
as if he had known Sarah very well indeed. Anne
took a breath, reminding herself that she must not
jump to conclusions. It could be nothing. And
yet . . .

"Actually it is a portrait of my mother, done during her first Season. But they were much alike, as

you can see for yourself." Her tone was matter-of-fact, giving no hint of her inner trepidation.

"Of course." Captain Montgomery shook his head, as if trying to clear his thoughts. "Miss Webster, I presume?"

"Yes."

"Captain Alistair Montgomery, at your service," he said with a stiff bow. "I am grateful to you for seeing me. I have a confidential matter that I need to discuss with you."

"Yes?" she asked, her curiosity aroused.

Captain Montgomery looked around, his glance taking in the open door, the housemaid busily polishing the woodwork outside and the footman who had taken it upon himself to trim the candles in the hall. "Is there somewhere we could be private?"

It was an impertinent request. Yet he did not have the look of a lecher. Rather he looked like a man who had steeled himself to deliver ill tidings.

"Does this concern Sarah?"

He nodded.

Anne went over to the door. "Tess, Adam, I am certain you are needed elsewhere," she said. Then she closed the door.

"Pray, have a seat," she invited.

Two chairs flanked the fireplace. She walked over and sat down in one, indicating that the captain was to sit in the other. As he did so, she gathered her composure. She had the most dreadful suspicion that she knew what he was going to tell her.

Captain Montgomery perched on his seat awkwardly, as if he would rather be anywhere else other than here. He steepled his hands before him and stared at them in apparent fascination.

The silence stretched between them. "Go on," she said when she could bear it no longer.

"I know what I have to tell you may shock you, but I ask you to hear me out before you pass judgment."

Anne nodded, afraid to trust her voice.

"Nearly seven years ago, when I was a young lieutenant, my ship was sent to Lower Canada. I was dispatched on special duty to the provincial capital. There I met your sister." He paused for a moment, his eyes unfocused as if he were remembering that occasion. "She was the most beautiful woman I had ever seen, and yet she seemed dreadfully unhappy. Her husband, Colonel Fitzwilliam, had been away for months. And even when he was there, he was not given to warm feelings or shows of affection."

Anne began to grow angry. "So you decided to comfort her," she said venomously.

Captain Montgomery flushed, but he met her gaze squarely. "It was not like that. We were friends. That is, I daresay she saw me as a friend. I was head over heels in love. I know it is shameful, but I kept thinking that if her husband were killed and she were free . . ."

He paused, swallowing hard. "Then one night, a madness came over us. I don't know how else to explain it. She asked me to escort her home from a party at the Governor's house. When I did, she invited me in. One thing led to another, and that night she let me make love to her."

"I think I have heard quite enough," Anne said, rising from her chair.

"Stay," he barked, in a voice of command. "Please," he added in a softer tone.

Anne resumed her seat, curious in spite of herself.

"It was only the one night," he said. "We both realized it had been a dreadful mistake. We agreed not to see each other again. I called in some favors and was given orders to rejoin my ship. I never saw her again."

"And you expect me to believe this?"

"As God is my witness, I tell you this is the truth."

She looked at him, as if she could read the truth of his words by his face and manner. His story matched what few details Sarah had let slip in her final days. "But why did you not attempt to contact her family before? Where were you when Sarah needed you?"

"She never sent word, though the navy would have forwarded any message she sent. In time I learned of her death, and though I mourned her, I had put that evening firmly from my mind. For many years I was at sea, returning to England only rarely. And then this spring, by chance, I encountered an acquaintance I had made in Canada. He gave me news that greatly disturbed me. And now I have come to you to see if the rumors are true." He leaned forward, focusing all his attention on her. "Tell me, Miss Webster. Was there a child?"

Anne did not know what to say or think. Over the years she had pictured Ian's father as a heartless rake. She had never expected to be face-to-face with him. Nor had she expected that the villain would come in the guise of an earnest gentleman.

"Yes. There was a babe," she said, choosing her words carefully.

Captain Montgomery sagged back in the chair as if the life had drained out of him. "I did not know," he said. "Oh, Sarah. Why did you not send for me? If I had only been there . . ."

It was clear that he believed the story Sarah's husband had spread, that her child had died at birth. Anne knew she could tell him to leave and that he would go. A part of her argued that he did not deserve to know more.

And if he had been the rake she had expected, she would have held her tongue and sent him on his way. But her instincts told her Captain Montgomery was no rake. He seemed genuinely distraught to hear of Sarah's pregnancy and the loss of her child. Which made it all the more strange that Sarah had kept the news of her pregnancy from him.

Perhaps she had been trying to protect him, knowing that the scandal would ruin him just as surely as it had ruined her. She may even have been in love with him, finding in the young naval officer what she had not found in her marriage. But whatever secrets had been in Sarah's heart, she had taken them with her to the grave. Now it was up to Anne to decide what was best for all concerned.

"The child was a boy. She named him Ian."

Captain Montgomery blinked back what looked suspiciously like tears. "Ian was my brother's name. He was killed at the battle of Alexandria," he said softly.

It was the sign she needed. Sarah must have cared for this man, to have named their child after his brother.

"I have something to tell you, but before I do so, I want your promise that you will not act on this information in any way unless you have my permission. Do you agree?" She would not reveal Ian's existence until she was certain she could protect him.

"How can I agree, if I don't know what you are asking?"

"Simply give me your word. You owe me that much. If not for me, then for Sarah's sake."

He winced. "I promise. Whatever you ask, if it is in my power I will do it."

She hesitated, but in the end decided there was nothing she could do except trust that he was indeed a man of honor. "I am sure you have heard that the child was stillborn," she said. "In truth, Colonel Fitzwilliam put the story about, to bury his shame."

It took a moment for her words to sink in. Then Captain Montgomery sat bolt upright, as if electrified. "You mean Ian is alive? Do you know where he is?"

"Of course. He lives here with me."

He jumped to his feet. "You must take me to him. At once."

"No."

"But—"

"No," Anne repeated firmly. "If you saw him, what would you tell him?"

"Why that I am his father, of course."

"Precisely. And that is why you can not see him."

Captain Montgomery argued, but Anne would not be swayed. She reminded him of his promise. He accused her of tricking him, then apologized for his rash words. He cajoled and pleaded, appealing to her compassion and invoking a father's right to his children.

At last Anne relented. "I will let you see him. But

only if you agree to let me introduce you as an acquaintance. Nothing more."

"Agreed." She knew he would have promised anything for a glimpse of his son.

She summoned a footman and instructed him to bring Ian to them. Her nerves jangling, she nearly called the servant back. But before she could do so, Ian appeared.

She had combed his hair only that morning, but from the tangles in his carrot-colored locks one would think he had not seen a comb or brush in a week. And he must have been playing with his tin soldiers, for the knees of his breeches had faint circles of dust. She fought the urge to apologize for Ian's appearance. There was nothing she needed to explain to Captain Montgomery.

Ian's eyes widened as he caught sight of their visitor.

As the lad came into the room, Captain Montgomery stood and Anne rose as well.

"Ian, this is Captain Montgomery of the Royal Navy. Captain, this is my son, Ian Webster."

Ian ducked his head in an awkward bow.

"I am very pleased to make your acquaintance, Master Ian."

"Thank you," Ian said.

He glanced from the captain to Anne and then back again, seeming to sense the tension between them.

"Since the captain is visiting today, I thought you would like to join us for tea," Anne said, by way of explanation.

"Yes, Mama," Ian said. He came over to stand beside her, careful to keep her between himself and their guest.

She led the way across the hall into the green salon, where the servants had already set out the tea tray. Anne chose a seat on the chintz sofa and drew Ian down beside her. The captain sat opposite them.

It was the most uncomfortable half-hour of her life. True to his word, the captain said nothing to Ian indicating he was anything more than a casual visitor. But he could not disguise the hunger in his eyes when he looked at his son. Still, they both tried to behave as if nothing was amiss.

Ian gradually warmed to the captain, peppering him with questions about life at sea. Having made the journey from Canada to England, Ian considered himself an expert sailor. Ian was briefly disappointed when the captain confirmed Anne's assertion that a boy of six was too young to join the navy, but managed to console himself with a second cream cake.

Anne breathed a prayer of relief when tea was finished and she was able to send Ian away.

"He is a fine boy," Captain Montgomery said, once they were both alone.

"Yes."

"He calls you Mama." It was not quite a question.

"As you heard. He knows his real mother was my sister, but when she died I became his new mother."

"It is quite a thing for an unmarried woman to take on a child."

She had known that it would not take him long to reach the obvious conclusion. "As you have no doubt guessed, most people assume that Ian is my natural child. Colonel Fitzwilliam buried the scandal very well."

"I admire your compassion, but you should never had had to bear this burden. The responsibility is mine."

"Ian is not a duty or a responsibility," Anne argued. "I love him as my own son."

"Indeed. But now it is time for me to do my share, and to make amends for the past. I can think of nothing that would give me more pleasure than for my wife and I to raise Ian as our own."

"Your wife?" Had she been mistaken in his character?

"Yes. We were married two years ago," he said quickly.

"Ah."

"Well, will you consider my offer?"

She did not need time to think. "No. Ian is as dear to me as if he were truly my son. I will not turn him over to strangers."

"I understand how much you care for him. But you must think of what is best for Ian. He would have a loving family, and benefit from a father's guidance. I would adopt him and claim him publicly as my own. I would ensure that he lacks for nothing."

"He lacks for nothing now."

"Except a father's love. How can you deny him the chance to know his only living parent?"

"So you say now. But what will your wife think? How can you expect her to raise your bastard child? Will she not wish to protect her own children?"

He flinched. "We have no children. And after last year's stillbirth, the doctors have told me that my wife will never bear a child. Ian is my son. The only son I will ever have. You can not be so cruel as to keep him from me."

She found herself pitying him. His anguish seemed sincere. But no words could convince her to part with Ian.

"I am the only family Ian has ever known. I will not deprive him of that."

"He has another family. He deserves the chance to know us."

She shook her head. "My mind is made up. I told you of Ian only because I knew that someday you would find out. It was best that you learn the truth from me and see for yourself that he is being well cared for."

Captain Montgomery thought for a moment. "If you will not do this for Ian's sake, then what of your own? You said yourself your reputation has suffered. Let me acknowledge Ian as my son. Once the truth is known, your reputation will be restored."

She realized that if Captain Montgomery claimed Ian as his own, she would be free to marry Freddie. But as soon as the thought occurred, she was ashamed of herself. How could she be so selfish, to think of her own happiness over Ian's?

"If Sarah had wanted you to raise Ian, she would have sent for you," Anne said harshly. "But she did not. She gave him into my care. And my mind is firm on this."

"Wait," Captain Montgomery said, clearly recognizing the value of a strategic retreat. "Do not make a decision in haste. I realize my coming here has been a shock. I will give you time to consider what is best for Ian."

She wished a thousand times over that she had never told him of Ian's existence. If only she could turn back the clock and leave the words unsaid. But they had been spoken. And now she had to deal with the consequences.

"I will think about what you have said." But no matter of thought would change her answer. She would never let Ian go. Not for anything.

Thirteen

Freddie's mind was filled with thoughts of Anne, but try though he did, it was midafternoon before he was able to escape from Beechwood Park. It seemed there were a hundred things which required his personal attention. First, he had to bid a courteous farewell to those guests who were leaving, including his sister Elizabeth and her husband David Rutledge. He was genuinely sorry to see them go.

Most of his other guests had chosen to remain through the weekend. He was disappointed, but not surprised, that Miss Sommersby and her parents were not among those who were departing.

Then he had to confer with the illuminators who had staged last night's spectacle. They insisted on his touring the grounds, to prove that no lasting harm had been done by the fireworks. Only then would they accept their fee.

Every time he turned around, it seemed there was someone requiring his attention. Servants, with questions about restoring the grand room after the ball. Guests, who wished to compliment him on last night's entertainments. Young men, in search of Priscilla.

Through it all he somehow managed to remain civil, though it took every ounce of his patience. Couldn't they realize that he had more important things on his mind than deciding what to do with the wine that had been opened but not drunk last night? Every delay meant another minute that kept him from Anne, and from hearing her say that she would be his wife.

At last he managed to free himself from his obligations. He simply refused to answer any more questions, pretending that he was deaf. Even then, one of the servants followed him right to the stables, until it became clear that his master had no intention of returning to the house to answer Lady Frederick's summons.

When he was shown into the library, he found Anne pacing across the carpet. She turned when she heard him enter, but she did not smile, nor did she rush to greet him.

"Anne, what is wrong?"

"Nothing."

He crossed the distance that separated them, and took her hands in his, giving them a gentle squeeze. As he drew closer he could see her eyes were rimmed in red, as if she had been crying. "Come now, you can tell me. What is troubling you?"

She disengaged her hands from his, and drew back a pace. "It is nothing. Nothing that you can help me with."

"This has to do with your last caller," he said. As he had ridden up, he had encountered a naval officer who apparently had just been leaving. Freddie would have sworn the man was a stranger, yet there had been something familiar in his appearance.

Anne's head jerked up. "What did he say?"

"He merely bid me good day and rode on."

Anne sighed in apparent relief.

"Who was he?" Freddie asked.

Anne turned away and, with one hand, began tracing the carvings on the side of the fireplace. "I do not wish to talk about him," she said.

He could not understand what was happening. Anne had never before refused to confide in him. She had even trusted him with the story of Ian's birth. What possible secret could there be that she could not bear to share with him?

"Was that Ian's father?"

He expected her to deny it, but instead she nodded, looking old beyond her years.

"What did he want?"

"Nothing," she said, but they both knew it for a lie.

The man who had sired Ian would not have come on a mere social visit. There had been a reason for his appearance, and whatever that reason was, it had clearly distressed Anne.

"Anne, there must be something I can do to help. Even if it is only to listen." He would do anything for her, even challenge the captain to a duel, if only she would turn to him for help.

"No," she said. "I must make this decision on my own."

There was only one explanation for her coldness toward him. "Are you angry about last night? Do you wish me to apologize?"

"Apologize? Whatever for?"

"For kissing you."

"Oh. That."

A wave of humiliation crashed over him. How could she have forgotten so easily what they had shared? Had it truly been that forgettable for her?

"I apologize if I took liberties," he said.

"There is no need." A faint flush rose on her cheeks. Her tongue traced her lips as if remembering the sensations of last night. But he knew that it was an unconscious gesture, and not an invitation to repeat those pleasures. Anne was too tense for him to risk such a gesture. He did not know how she would respond.

Last night he had felt so close to her. And today, it was as if a stranger had taken her place.

If only she was his. If they were married, or even simply engaged, then he would have a right to share her troubles and to protect her from whatever or whomever was troubling her.

"So, have you thought about my proposal?" he asked.

"No. Yes. I mean it is too soon for me to give you an answer."

"What is there to think about?"

Her eyes sparked with anger, and he knew it had been the wrong thing to say.

"One embrace is hardly the basis for deciding the rest of our lives," she retorted. "There is more than our own happiness to consider. I must think of Ian and of what is best for all of us."

He heard the anger in her words, the unhappiness that lay underneath. It made him feel like the lowest of worms. "Anne, I am sorry if I pressed you. You know how I feel. I want to make you happy, to give you and Ian a home. But you can take all the time you need to decide."

"Thank you," she said.

He hoped she would invite him to tea or offer to confide in him. But she did not. There was a strain between them that he had never felt before. He wondered frantically what the man had said to cause such a change in Anne. What secret did she hold so tightly within her that caused her such misery?

Anne had always confided in him, yet now she held herself apart from him. He could see it in the stiffness of her carriage, the way her eyes refused to meet his.

He could press her for answers, but he would not. He did not want to jeopardize their relationship. Let her see that he trusted her. In time she would turn to him for help.

"I can see you are distressed, so I will take my leave," he said. "But please, if there is anything I can do, do not hesitate to send for me. Anything at all."

Unwilling to leave without some token of affection, he bent forward and kissed her cheek. She did not pull away, but neither did she return his gesture. He left, barely able to contain his disappointment. His one consolation was the sure knowledge that this was just a temporary setback. Today, she had been understandably troubled, but he knew that once she recovered her equilibrium, things would be as before and she would agree to be his wife.

* * *

That night, when Anne went to tuck Ian into bed, she found him in an unusually pensive mood. Unlike most nights, he did not protest when told it was time for bed, but instead obediently climbed right in. Smoothing back the hair from his face, she felt his forehead, but it did not seem warm. Perhaps he was simply tired.

"Mama, will you tell me a story?"

"One story," she said, seating herself on the bed beside him. She could not help but think how small and fragile he looked in that big bed.

She cast her mind about and then began. "A long time ago in a land called Greece—"

"No," he interrupted. "I want to hear about my mother. My real mother."

"Very well," she said, wondering what had prompted him to ask for this story. It had been months since he had asked about his mother. Still, if it would make him happy . . . "From the day she was born, your mother Sarah was the most beautiful girl the county had ever seen. She was graceful and well mannered, and her father called her his little princess."

"Because she had golden hair," Ian interjected.

"That's right. And when she grew up, she married and moved far across the sea to Canada. She was very lonely there, especially after her husband left to fight in the wars. So she made a mistake, and found another man to take his place. Then he left. She was sad, but then she discovered she was to have you."

"And she wouldn't be lonely anymore," Ian added, impatient with Anne's slow telling of the tale.

"Yes, but after you were born she was very sick.

So she gave you to me. She knew I would love you just as if you were my own true child," she said, giving him a fierce hug.

"My mama is in heaven with the angels?"

"Yes," Anne said, hoping that it was true.

"But what about my father?"

"I don't know," she said. "Perhaps he is dead and could not come for you." The words were bitter on her tongue. It was the answer she had always given him, but now it was a lie. What would Ian think if he knew that his father was alive and that moreover he had met him this very day? Would he be thrilled to meet the man he had so long imagined? Or would he be hurt and angry that it had taken so long for his father to find him?

Someday Ian would learn the truth. If not from her, then surely from some other. What would he think of her then? Would he thank her for protecting him? Or resent her for robbing him of the years he could have spent getting to know his father?

"Mama, will Lord Frederick be my new father?"

"Where on earth did you get that idea?"

"I heard Cook talking. She said Freddie wants to make an honest woman of you. That means getting married," he explained earnestly. "If you marry Lord Frederick, does that make him my father?"

"I have not agreed to marry anyone," Anne said.

"But you should marry him," Ian said. "He knows all sorts of things. And he never makes me feel like a nuisance."

If only matters were as simple as they seemed to a six-year-old mind.

"Well, I am glad you like him," Anne said. "But

it is too soon to be talking marriage. And you, young man, have to get to sleep. You had a busy day today."

"Yes, Mama," Ian said.

Anne kissed him good night and left the room, knowing that Ian would be asleep in minutes. How she envied his untroubled conscience. For herself, she had much to consider, and she doubted very much that sleep would come.

Fourteen

The next days were difficult for Anne. Captain Montgomery called on her twice, urging her to reconsider her decision. At last he left, to return to his duties in Portsmouth. But she knew that he had not given up the idea of raising Ian as his own. He was merely giving her time to reflect.

Harder still to bear was the separation from Freddie. She longed to and yet dreaded to see him again. A part of her wanted his advice, wanted the chance to share the burden of this decision with him. But another part urged her to keep her silence. How could she trust his judgment when she could not trust her own? If Freddie sided with Captain Montgomery, would it be because he truly believed a father had a right to his son? Or would his advice be based on the knowledge that by sending Ian away, she would be removing the taint of scandal from her and his own family?

She could not trust him. She did not trust herself. She loved Ian as much as if he were truly her own son. And yet, when Captain Montgomery had offered to adopt him, for one moment she had been tempted, knowing that relinquishing Ian would free her to marry Freddie. It was a selfish impulse, banished as quickly as the thought occurred. And though she knew it was irrational, she blamed Freddie for her current dilemma. If he had not proposed, she would never have been tempted by Captain Montgomery's offer.

Her thoughts ran round and round in circles. At one moment she knew that the wisest course was to return to Canada, where she and Ian could resume their lives as if nothing had occurred. She would give up a chance for marriage to Freddie, but she would also distance herself from Captain Montgomery.

Yet as soon as she fixed her mind on that course of action, she found herself wondering what it would be like to be the captain, to know you had a son and that you could not acknowledge him. Did she have the moral right to keep Ian from his father? And what was best for Ian? That he grow up never knowing his father? Was it better to be a bastard of unknown origin? Or would it be easier for him if he was acknowledged by his father?

Natural children were not unheard of in society. There were even a few ladies who accepted the tangible evidence of their husband's indiscretions into their households, raising those children along with his legitimate offspring. And while they never achieved equal status with legitimate offspring, they were often far better off than they would have been elsewhere. Of course, Ian's situation would be even better. With no possibility of legitimate offspring, Captain Montgomery would be free to declare Ian his heir.

The arrival of Boswell with the morning post was

a welcome distraction from her thoughts. He placed the letters on the desk in the sitting room and then retreated a pace.

"Yes?" she asked.

"Cook wishes to know if there will be any guests for tea today."

Anne grimaced. Freddie had sent over a footman with a message, inviting her to go riding. She had sent back a curt no, not willing to face him. Not now.

"Not today," she said firmly.

"Very good," Boswell said. His expression was impassive but he could not hide the flicker of speculation in his eyes. She knew that he, along with the rest of the staff, was puzzled by the recent turn of events. No doubt they knew that Freddie had offered marriage and that she had refused to give him an answer. From their point of view, her actions must seem incredibly foolish. Yet she felt no need to enlighten them.

As Boswell left the room, she turned her attention to the stack of letters he had left behind.

The first was from her solicitor Mr. Creighton. Obedient to the instructions she had given him weeks ago, he now wrote to say that he had found a tenant interested in renting the property, beginning in October. If she was still of a mind to return to Canada, although he advised against it, then she should inform him and he would finalize the arrangements for the lease. He ended the letter by reporting that he had completed the valuation of her father's estate and that the papers establishing the trust for Ian would be ready to sign within the fortnight.

It was another reminder that her time was running out. It was already late August. If she wished to leave England, they would have to sail within the month, to avoid the autumn storms. She set the letter aside. She could give Mr. Creighton no answer until she had determined the course of her own future.

Anne turned next to a letter addressed in an unfamiliar hand. She unfolded it, and discovered that it was from Mrs. Montgomery, the captain's wife. Mrs. Montgomery wrote that she had always longed for children and had been devastated when the doctors had told her it was not to be. Learning of Ian's existence was the answer to her prayers. She had forgiven her husband for his youthful indiscretion, and could think of nothing more fitting than that she and her husband raise Ian. Understanding Anne's natural caution, she suggested that Anne and Ian should come on a visit to Portsmouth. She was certain that once Anne was better acquainted with them, she would be able to make the right decision.

Anne stuffed the letter in the pocket of her gown. Then, without pausing to don a bonnet, she went out into the August sunshine. She strode quickly across the grounds, not with any particular direction in mind, just knowing that she needed to keep moving. If she was moving she did not have to think. Eventually her steps slowed as she found herself approaching the oak tree that stood near the stream. Images flashed through her mind. Freddie smiling as he teased her into fits of the giggles. Freddie with Ian, teaching him to skip pebbles across the stream. Freddie sitting on the ground beside her, suddenly serious, as he spoke of how much he had missed her.

Strange that her feet had led her to this, of all spots. Feeling the sun beat down on her head, she took shelter under the tree. Then, seating herself on the grass, she withdrew the letter and read it again.

She tried to think about Mrs. Montgomery's offer. But instead her mind turned to the last time Freddie had joined them for an afternoon. After playing a frantic game of tag with Ian, he had returned to her and thrown himself full length on the grass in apparent exhaustion. She had teased him, saying that she sometimes had difficulty remembering whether it was Ian or Freddie who was the six-year-old boy. Freddie had replied that it was simply because he had not forgotten what it was to be six. And then his mood had turned solemn. "What that boy needs is a father," he had said. "Every boy needs a man to guide him." She had known that he was speaking from experience. Freddie's own father had died when he was a mere boy of seven, and in some ways Freddie had never recovered from that loss.

A boy needs a father. She repeated the words to herself, and in that instant she realized she had decided she would accept Mrs. Montgomery's invitation. She would give herself the chance to become acquainted with the Montgomerys before she decided what role they would play in Ian's life.

Freddie was stunned.

Anne had left him. She had gone, without telling him where. All he had was a note from her, saying that she had left to attend to an urgent matter. She did not say where she was going or why. And she had instructed her servants not to deliver the note until the day after her departure.

Clearly she did not want him to follow her. And questioning her servants had proven fruitless. All they could tell him was that the groom had driven Anne to Watertown. From there she had presumably taken the stage.

His hand reached up, smoothed the breast pocket which held her note. All he had to cling to were her closing lines. She had promised to speak with him upon her return. And she had signed the note, "Yours, affectionately, Anne."

It did not take a genius to realize that her sudden trip was somehow linked to the naval captain who had visited her. But what would cause her to leave? What secret was there between them, a secret she could not reveal to her oldest and dearest friend?

She had confirmed that the mysterious captain was Ian's father. But that revelation alone would not account for her sudden coldness toward him or her leaving without a word. In his mind he heard a voice telling him that Anne's behavior was that of a guilty woman, one who knew that her secret was about to be exposed. With her lover's return, Anne could no longer pretend that Ian was Sarah's illegitimate child.

Even her own father had believed the boy to be Anne's. And now her disappearance, coming hard on the heels of the captain's visit, was proof enough of her guilt. Only a fool would still believe in Anne's innocence.

The voice in his head sounded very much like that of his mother. He ignored it, putting all his faith in Anne. He trusted her word. She had told him the truth about Ian, and if she had written that she would return, then he would trust that she would do so.

And in part he blamed himself. He never should have left Anne that day, with things so unsettled between them. He should have stayed and fought for himself. Convinced Anne to share her troubles. No matter what they were, anything would be better than this uncertainty. He vowed that when Anne returned he would not let her go until he convinced her to marry him. He would plead his case with gentle logic and sweet kisses.

And if that did not work, perhaps he could convince her that she had compromised him and must marry him to save his honor. The ghost of a smile touched his lips. Now there was an argument she could not refuse.

"It is about time you started smiling," his mother said. "You have been moping about the house like gloom personified. This melancholy is ill becoming in you. I don't know what your guests must be thinking."

Freddie turned and saw his mother standing in the doorway of his dressing room. Was there no peace to be had these days? His dressing room and bedroom were the only places he could be certain that he would not be pursued by his guests. But, of course, the Dowager Lady Frederick had no qualms about intruding on her son's privacy.

"They are Priscilla's guests, not mine. For my part, I will be glad to see their backs when they leave."

"You should not say such a thing."

He sighed. "Most of the guests are a tolerable sort,

and they serve to keep Priscilla amused. It is merely Miss Sommersby and her parents that I object to."

His mother came into the room and shut the door behind her. "Miss Sommersby is a perfectly unexceptionable young woman."

"So she is," he agreed. "And she would be pleasant company, did she not fancy herself as the next Viscountess Frederick. I have tried to make my position plain to her"—his gaze locked on to his mother's—"but it seems someone has been encouraging her ambitions."

"It was not all that long ago that you thought she would make an excellent viscountess. After all you proposed to her."

So. She had known about the marriage offer. He had suspected as much, but this was the first time she had admitted it.

"Miss Sommersby did me the greatest of services by refusing my offer. I will be forever in her debt," he said.

"Nonsense. That is just your pride speaking. Miss Sommersby will make you an excellent wife. She has breeding, fortune and pleasing manners. She is modest and well behaved, and young enough that you can mold her character."

He repressed a shudder. It sounded as if he were picking a horse, not a partner to spend the rest of his life with.

"Since she is such a paragon, I am certain she will not lack for other suitors. As for me, I have already chosen the woman I intend to marry."

His mother blanched. "Tell me it is not that dreadful Webster chit."

"I have asked Anne Webster to be my wife. She has not yet agreed, but in time she will."

His mother sank down on the chair in front of the dressing table. "Do not do this. Think of your family. Think of your sister Priscilla. Who will want to marry into a family touched by such scandal?" Her voice trembled with anger. "Seven generations of Fredericks have lived their lives in honor, only to be brought down by this shame."

She was exaggerating, of course, but he felt a stab of guilt, for he could see that his mother was truly distraught. "I hardly think it will come to that. But if there is a scandal, we will live it down. In time it will all be forgotten."

He knelt down on one knee beside her chair. And though she rarely permitted him to touch her, this once he placed his right hand on her shoulder. "Mother, marrying Anne will make me the happiest of men. For once, I am choosing happiness over duty. Can you not find it in your heart to wish us well?"

She picked up his hand and removed it from her shoulder. "Never," she said with fierce determination. "I will never accept this travesty."

Her rejection stung. He had tried to consider her feelings, but it was clear she had no consideration for his. "I mean to have Anne as my wife, and I will not let you come between us. If you can not reconcile yourself to this match, then I am certain you will be far happier residing elsewhere."

His mother stood up, shaking her skirts as if to shake off the contamination of his presence. "You will do what you must. And I will do what I must." And with that she left the room.

He stared at her retreating form. His mother's disapproval would cast a heavy shadow on his marriage. Particularly if she took it into her head to make public her dislike of Anne. He could only hope that she would see reason. After all, if she estranged herself from him permanently, she would never know his children. And while she had grandchildren in plenty, only Freddie's son would be the next Viscount Frederick.

His lips curved up in a smile, as he pictured how it would feel to have his own children. He could not imagine any more happiness than starting his own family with Anne, with Ian as the older brother to the other youngsters. He already knew that Anne would make a good mother, and he hoped fervently that he would make a good father as well. Even if his mother and every member of society refused to accept them, so be it. As long as he had Anne, he needed no one else.

Fifteen

Anne paused on the sidewalk, checking the letter in her hand. The direction was clearly written. Number sixteen, New King's Street, Portsmouth. When she and Ian had arrived in Portsmouth last night, she had debated over sending word to the Montgomerys, but then had decided that she would simply call in person. A hired carriage had taken her to New King's Street. Number sixteen proved to be one of a row of new town houses built out of the gray stone that was native to the area. It was a very respectable address. Far more than an ordinary naval officer could afford. Captain Montgomery or his wife must be well connected indeed. The thought did not bring her comfort.

She gave herself a mental shake. She could not stand there, mooning about. There was nothing she need be afraid of. Steeling her nerves, she marched up the steps and rapped with the brass door knocker.

The door was opened by a maid. "May I help you?"

"I wish to see Mrs. Montgomery."

The maid looked at her expectantly, and Anne realized that she was waiting for a card. In the or-

dinary course of things, no gentlewoman would be
without a calling card. But Anne had never needed
them before.

"Tell her Miss Webster is here. I am certain she
will wish to see me."

The maid gave Anne a look that sized her up,
then opened the door wide. "Please, come in and
wait here. I will see if my mistress is at home."

Anne stood in the hallway as the maid disappeared
upstairs. A moment later, the maid returned, followed by a woman in her mid twenties who could
only be Mrs. Montgomery. Her modestly cut gown
showed a figure that was a shade plumper than current fashion, but the printed muslin was of the first
quality. Framed by fine blond hair, her round face
seemed made for smiles, but the expression it bore
now was one of caution.

"Miss Webster?" she asked.

"Yes."

"I am Mrs. Montgomery. I am very pleased to
make your acquaintance." Mrs. Montgomery extended her hand for Anne to shake. Then she
looked behind Anne, as if expecting someone else
to be there.

"I came alone," Anne said, realizing that Mrs.
Montgomery was looking for Ian.

"Of course," Mrs. Montgomery said, although
Anne could tell she was disappointed. "My husband
is at the Naval Yards. I could send a servant for
him . . ."

"I thought it best if the two of us talked. Alone,"
Anne said. It was why she had decided to call unan-
nounced rather than sending word ahead. Without

the presence of her husband, Mrs. Montgomery might be more willing to speak her feelings.

"Certainly," Mrs. Montgomery replied. "If you will follow me, I have a tolerable sitting room in the back. Dora, please bring refreshments for our guest."

Even for August, it was an unmercifully hot day. It was the kind of day that should be spent indoors, or at least by the shores of some convenient lake. No sensible person would have chosen this as the day for an excursion.

Unfortunately sensible was the last word that could be applied to this house party. Priscilla, having spent days planning an excursion to view the stone circle at Emlyn's Leap, was not to be denied her treat. "What is a little sun, when compared with the chance to see stones that have stood since the time of Arthur?" she had exclaimed. "Every time I am there I feel a mystic connection to the glories of the past. How can we deny our guests a chance to share in such an experience?"

She had sighed with rapturous delight. The Misses Crane had declared their fervent desire to sketch the prospect. The gentlemen, while immune to the glories of the past, had no objection to a plan that allowed them to spend an entire day with the ladies.

Even Lady Frederick, who in the normal course of affairs could be counted on to restrain Priscilla's enthusiastic starts, declared herself in favor of the idea, and announced her intention to go on the excursion herself. Freddie could not help wondering what prompted her sudden interest in the stone circle. She had lived in the county for over thirty years, and to the best of his knowledge she had never before expressed an interest in ruins of any sort.

In vain Freddie pointed out all the attendant discomforts of such an excursion. The circle was more than two hours away. It would be a long journey, made during the hottest part of the day. Moreover the stones themselves, while of local interest, were hardly to be compared to the great stone circles, such as the one in Salisbury Plain.

Eventually, however, he allowed himself to be persuaded. After all, the guests were leaving tomorrow. All he had to do was avoid Miss Sommersby's company for one more day, and then he would be free. If he remained at home he was certain she would invent some excuse for staying behind, while in such a large party, it would be easier to avoid being alone with Miss Sommersby. And with Anne absent, there was no reason for him to remain.

In the end there were an even dozen in the party that left to view the stone circle. The ladies were his mother, Priscilla, the two sisters Crane, Lady Alice, Miss Flockhart and Miss Sommersby. And for the gentlemen, in addition to himself there was Mr. Arthur Crane, Ensign Bisland, Mr. Chumley and their neighbor Charles Dunne. All unexceptionable, except for Arthur Crane who had taken to following Priscilla about like a lovesick puppy. Fortunately she did not seem to take him seriously.

Although the idea was Priscilla's, it was Lady Frederick who organized the expedition with her usual efficiency. A quartet of servants was sent ahead with a cart full of provisions, to prepare an alfresco luncheon. There were three carriages to

convey the ladies and those gentlemen who chose
not to ride. Freddie, wary of a long journey with
Miss Sommersby, announced his intention to ride
Ajax.

The journey proved every bit as uncomfortable as
he had foreseen. Some of the younger gentlemen
chose to ride alongside the carriages containing the
ladies, but for his part Freddie was content to ride
in silence at the rear of the procession. The heat
beat down unmercifully upon them. He could feel
his brains baking in his skull, yet knew better than
to suggest they cancel the expedition. There would
be no shade or rest until they reached the stone
circle.

At last they approached the village of Emlyn's
Leap. Freddie, after making certain that the rest of
the party knew the way, declared that he was riding
on ahead to ensure that all was in readiness for their
arrival.

Since the stone circle lay on the grounds of the
Farthingdale estate, Freddie stopped by the gatehouse and made the customary payment of a guinea
to the gatekeeper. Proceeding down the lane, a quarter-mile past the gatehouse he turned off onto the
path that wound through the oak woods. It was
blessedly shady under the trees, but the woods were
small and in a few moments he emerged back into
the sunlight.

The stone circle lay in a small meadow between
the oak woods and a river. It was a popular spot,
and the groundskeepers kept the meadow grass cut
short for the convenience of visitors. A path led to
the outskirts of the circle, around the stones and
then down to the river. A trail ran along the river-

bank. If one walked downriver the meadow was eventually swallowed up by the woods, but the trail was well marked, and half a mile downriver there was a waterfall.

The circle itself was made up of thirteen granite stones, the tallest of which stood no more than twice the height of a man. A stone had fallen over, and the rest leaned drunkenly. One in particular looked as if it might fall if given the slightest push. But appearances were deceptive. Despite all of Freddie's youthful efforts, the stone still stood.

Freddie dismounted, and led Ajax off to a corner of the meadow. Removing the bridle, he put the hobbles on and set Ajax free to graze.

A respectful distance from the circle, the servants had set out small tables draped with linen and had placed chairs around them. There would be no casual lounging around on the ground, not while Lady Frederick was in charge. The assistant cook watched a small fire, while the three footmen busied themselves setting out the refreshments. Seeing that all was in readiness, Freddie set himself to wait for the arrival of the others.

The rest of the party arrived only a few minutes later. Priscilla proudly showed off the circle as if she had constructed it herself. She related various fanciful histories of the site and then concluded with her favorite tale. "And in the time of King William, there lived a great Norman lord. He had one daughter, Mathilda, said to be the fairest woman in all of England. One day she was walking in the woods with her ladies when she met Sir Emlyn. He had been a Saxon knight, but had lost all his lands and properties to the Normans and now lived in the woods.

They fell in love at the instant, and they began to
meet secretly here at the stone circle. All was well
until one of her ladies betrayed her and told her
father. He was enraged. When Emlyn came to the
circle, he was met, not by his lady but by her father
and his knights. Emlyn ran for his life, till they surrounded him by the waterfall. Rather than be captured, he leapt over the cliff and was killed. When
Mathilda learned of her lover's death, she killed herself as well. But every midsummer's night their spirits return to the circle in remembrance of their
love."

"How thrilling!" exclaimed Lady Alice.

"How positively romantic," said the elder Miss
Crane.

The gentlemen were less impressed. "What kind
of a man was he to run like that?" asked Ensign
Bisland. "A real man would have stood his ground
rather than fleeing like a dog."

Priscilla gave the young ensign a scornful glance.
"Humph! You have not a romantic bone in your
body." She ostentatiously turned her back on him.

"You tell the story so well I can almost see them,"
Arthur Crane said to Priscilla.

She dimpled up at him. "Do you really think so?"

"Indeed."

"Well, I have more stories I can tell," she said,
allowing Mr. Crane to take her arm. "And the ruins
of the castle are not far off in the woods. Perhaps
we could stroll there after we have our luncheon.
Did you know that the first . . . ?"

Freddie felt a stab of sympathy for Arthur Crane.
Little did the fool know, but Priscilla could talk for
hours.

The party strolled about the stone circle until
Lady Frederick summoned them to dine.

As the afternoon wore on, Freddie kept a wary
eye on the sky. The sun still beat down, but now the
pale blue sky was tinged with haze, and in the distance he could see a dark line of clouds. There was
a storm coming. But the clouds were to the west,
and Beechwood lay to the east. With luck, they
should be able to return home before the rain began.

The luncheon over, the servants began clearing
away the dishes, packing them away in the cart. The
party rose and began strolling about the meadow.
He saw his mother speaking first with Lady Alice
and then with Miss Sommersby. He waited until Miss
Sommersby moved off before approaching his
mother. "There will be rain soon," he said. "It
would be best if we left now."

"You may be right," she said.

"Oh, no! We can not leave now," said Priscilla.
"The storm is still far off. And I did so want to show
Mr. Crane the waterfall."

"I think we should depart," Freddie said firmly.

"You are panicking over nothing," Mr. Dunne
said. "Those clouds are miles away. It will be hours
before they are here, and who is to say whether or
not they will bring rain with them?"

Freddie looked around and realized he faced a
potential mutiny. He took a deep breath. He could
insist on their leaving. But he would not. If they
chose to ignore his advice, then so be it. It would
be no more than they deserved if they got caught
in the rain.

His mother gestured, and Priscilla came over to

where they were standing. "Lady Alice is not feeling well," his mother explained. Indeed, the poor woman seemed dreadfully pale. "I will be returning home with her and with Miss Sommersby. The rest of the party can follow later."

"Will you join us?" Priscilla asked Freddie.

"No. I have no wish to see the waterfall," he replied. He would see his mother off, then wait here until the rest of the party returned.

Priscilla joined her friends, and the gentlemen and ladies started down the path that led to the waterfall.

Freddie found the coachman and let him know that Lady Frederick wished to depart. Then he went over to check on the servants who were loading the last of the provisions into the cart. "You had best start back now," he instructed the assistant cook, Joseph. "I don't like the look of that sky."

"Yes, my lord," Joseph replied.

The heavily laden cart would travel more slowly than the carriages containing the party. But with any luck they would reach Beechwood before the rain broke.

He returned to see that the small curricle had been driven over to the edge of the circle. Lady Alice was seated within, while his mother stood beside it.

"Where is Miss Sommersby?" he asked.

"I do not know," Lady Frederick said. "She mentioned something about picking wildflowers, then wandered off in the direction of the woods. I thought she would be back in a moment, but the chit has not returned. You must go and find her."

His eyes narrowed. His mother had been maneu-

vering for days to place him alone with Miss Sommersby. This seemed like an unlikely coincidence.

"Why me?"

"Because there is no one else. The gentlemen are
all with Priscilla and her friends at the waterfall."

He hesitated; then his mother said sharply. "Just
go. Find the girl and bring her back. She can return
home with the rest of you."

At that moment Lady Alice gave a delicate moan
and pressed one hand to her stomach. She seemed
truly unwell. It was cruel of him to stand debating
with his mother while she was suffering.

"Lady Alice, I regret that you are not feeling well.
My mother is right. You should depart at once, and
the rest of the party will follow as soon as we may."

His mother gave him a rare smile of approval.

"Thank you," she said.

After they left, he paused for a moment to think.
If Miss Sommersby had intended to join the group
by the waterfall, she would have had to pass him as
he conferred with the cook. Therefore, she must
have followed the path upriver.

He began walking along the path. The river lay
to his left, while the woods lay to his right. The
woods gradually approached the path until he was
walking on their very boundary. Small white and yellow flowers bloomed along the edge of the woods,
and in the shade he could see wild primroses. "Miss
Sommersby," he called.

He continued to call her name as he walked, but
there was no response. Where on earth could the
chit have gone? Had she headed for the waterfall
after all? But no, he would have seen her. At last he
reached the spot where, as it emptied into the river,

a small stream cut across the path. The ground was muddy, and showed no signs of footprints. Very well. She had not come this way.

He retraced his steps, his irritation slowly turning to concern. If she had ventured off the trail, it would be very easy to become lost in the dense oak forest. Now he walked more slowly, his eyes searching the woods for any sign that a person had passed. Sure enough, after a quarter-mile he saw a small path that disappeared into the woods. A deer track, he guessed. There were no signs of footprints, but he decided it was worth investigating.

He ventured into the woods a couple of hundred yards. "Miss Sommersby," he called. He heard no answer and shouted again, with all the force he could muster "Miss Somm-ers-by!"

This time he heard a faint sound that might have been a reply. Ahead, and off to his left. Heading in that direction, he called again, and this time he could distinctly hear her calling.

He found her, sitting on the ground beside the ruins of an ancient stone tower. "Oh, my lord, I am so happy to see you," she exclaimed. "I have been here for simply hours."

He wondered why she did not stand when she saw him. He picked his way among the stones that had fallen to the ground over the years. "Miss Sommersby, is there something wrong?"

She blinked up at him, and he could see the tracks of tears on her face. "My ankle. I stumbled over those stones, and I think I broke it."

He gave her a sharp look. "Indeed. And just what were you doing here?"

"I thought I would bring some flowers back for

my mother," she said. "I started on the path, but
then I saw these glorious wild lilies in the woods. I
followed them in, and before I knew it, I was all
turned around. I kept calling and calling, but no
one came. Eventually I saw this tower. I knew it must
be the one from Priscilla's story. I thought I would
sit here and rest. But then I fell . . ."

Of all the stupid, foolish things. Even Priscilla
knew better than to wander off alone into unfamiliar
woods.

"We had best return to the others," he said. The
trees clustered thickly around the tower, but glancing directly up, he could see the sky had clouded
over.

He pulled his watch from his pocket. It was later
than he had thought. By now the others must have
returned from the waterfall. No doubt they were
wondering where he had disappeared to.

"Which ankle is it?"

"My right one," she said, pointing.

"Let me take a look at it."

He knelt down beside her. She gave a brief gasp
as his hand touched her ankle, and turned a bright
shade of crimson, whether from pain or modesty he
did not know.

"It does not feel broken," he said, trying to sound
more sure than he felt. "Let me help you to your
feet, and we will try walking."

She nodded.

He stood up and grasped both her hands in his,
then pulled her up till she was standing on her left
foot. Gingerly she put her right foot on the ground
and assayed a step. She moaned and would have
fallen if he had not caught her.

He wrapped his left arm around her waist. "Put your arm around my shoulders," he instructed. She raised her arm, and he stooped down so she could place it on his shoulders. "Now, let us try a step."

She hopped on her left foot. "There, you see? We can do it," he said encouragingly.

But they had not gone a half-dozen paces before she stumbled, and despite his best efforts she fell to the ground.

"Ouch!" she yelled.

"Are you all right?"

Tears welled up in her eyes, and she began to cry. "I am sorry. I am such a weakling," she said, "but I can not do it."

He looked down at her. She was right. At this pace, it would take them days to hop back to the clearing where the stone circle lay. He bent down on one knee and picked her up as if she were a child.

But she was no child, and he was barely able to stand upright with her in his arms. He would never be able to carry her the full distance. Not unless he tossed her over his shoulder, an act which would do nothing for either of their reputations.

He carried her the short distance back to the stone tower, and set her down on a convenient boulder. "I am afraid there is nothing else I can do. I must go for help," he said.

"No! You can not leave me," Miss Sommersby pleaded.

"I must. Do not worry, it will not be long," he promised. He turned and strode off.

As the sound of her pleading died off behind him, he realized that he wasn't quite sure how he had found the tower. He had been so focused on following Miss Sommersby's voice that he had not paid much attention to his surroundings. Game tracks crisscrossed the woods, and he tried to recall just which track he had followed in. Was it that one to the left? Hadn't he passed a fallen log just before he came into the clearing? Yes, that was it. Over there. As he started down the track, the rain began to fall. He sighed, but continued on, pausing every few paces to bend tree branches to point the way back.

He walked on as the rain grew heavier, and the light diminished until even he could see that there was no point in continuing on. With heavy heart he followed the trail of broken branches back to Miss Sommersby.

When he returned, he saw that she was not on the boulder where he had left her. "Miss Sommersby?"

"In here," she replied. He went inside the tower and found her sitting on the ground, leaning against the wall where the remnants of the original roof provided a modicum of shelter from the rain. Since she could not walk, she must have crawled in there, and he felt a stab of guilt for having left her alone.

She looked around. "Where are they?"

"They, er, I did not find them. And when the rain started, I thought it best to return here to see if you were all right."

Her lower lip trembled. "You mean we are lost?"

"We are not lost. I know where we are," he said testily. They were at the ruined tower. He just wasn't quite certain in which direction the river lay. But he was certain he could find it, as soon as the rain stopped. "Once the rain stops, I will start out again," he promised.

"What if it never stops?" she demanded. "Why haven't the others come to find us?"

"If they are sensible, they have sought shelter as we have."

"If they do not come soon, we will have to spend the night," she wailed. Her tears began again in earnest.

It was a conclusion he had reached himself. And he could not imagine a greater catastrophe. His reputation might just have survived being alone in the woods with Miss Sommersby, provided that he had found her quickly and just as expeditiously returned her to the others. But it had been hours now, and the rain showed no signs of letting up. She was already compromised. Spending the night together would just be the final nail in his coffin.

"This never would have happened if you hadn't wandered off on your own," he said angrily.

Miss Sommersby buried her face in her hands and continued crying. She shivered with the cold. He stripped off his own jacket and dropped it on her. "Put this on," he said gruffly. Then he found himself a seat, as far away from her as he could get and still be inside the tower.

She put on his jacket. It was absurdly large on her; the sleeves extended past her hands. Eventually she stopped crying and wiped her eyes with one sleeve before rolling both up.

"Better now?" he asked.

"Yes." She sniffed. "But there is no reason for you to be mean to me."

There was every reason in the world. Unless they

were discovered within the next hour, he would be honor-bound to marry this watering pot. He could not help wondering if this was indeed an unfortunate accident or if it was all part of some devious scheme.

"Tell me, Miss Sommersby," he said. "Whatever happened to Edward Farquhar?"

"The beast ruined my life. He told me he loved me, and then he ran off with that freckle-faced Mary Richmond. How could he do such a thing?"

Ah. So much for her true soul mate. No doubt Farquhar had hurt her and made her look foolish. Perhaps her pursuit of him stemmed from a desire to prove to everyone that she could do better than a wastrel like Farquhar. Still, she looked so forlorn that he could not help feeling sorry for her. "You are better off without him," he said, just as if she had been one of his sisters.

The rocks behind his back were uncomfortable. He shifted, trying to find a more suitable position. As he moved, the rain dripped down on him from the cracks in the roof. Eventually he gave up and resumed his old spot. He could hear the rain lashing against the tower walls and the occasional low rumble of distant thunder. The air in the tower smelled musty, as if animals had lived there once. But, looking around, he saw no recent sign of habitation.

"What should we do now?" she asked.

"Make yourself comfortable," he said. "We may be here a long while."

And as the darkness closed in, he found himself wondering how on earth he would break this dreadful news to Anne. For unless a miracle occurred, he would be forced to marry Miss Sommersby. He knew

Anne would understand that there was no other
honorable course. But would she ever forgive him?

And could he ever forgive himself?

His future stretched out before him, bleak and
empty.

Sixteen

During the night, the rain stopped. As the dawn broke, Freddie rose, his muscles protesting after the uncomfortable sleep. He shook Miss Sommersby awake so that she would not arise to find him gone. Then he set off. This time he was able to find his way to the river, and he followed the path to the stone circle.

There was no sign of Ajax. Nor was there any sign of the party, save for the small patch of ground where the cook fire had been. He debated walking to the main road, but decided it made better sense to wait here. Before an hour had passed, he heard the sound of a carriage.

"My lord!" exclaimed his coachman, John, as he drove into the clearing. "I am right glad to see you."

"And I you," Freddie replied. Would to God they had arrived yesterday.

In addition to the carriage, there were half-a-dozen grooms mounted on horses, no doubt to help search the woods.

John drew the carriage to a stop. "I wasn't sure if we would find you here. We have men checking every inn and cottage where you might have taken shelter."

The coachman's words extinguished any hope that they might be able to keep this matter private. With his servants beating the woods for him, everyone in the county would know what had happened before nightfall.

"And Miss Sommersby?" the coachman asked.

"She has injured her ankle," Freddie replied. He pointed to two of the grooms, "You two, follow me, and we will go fetch her. John, you can wait here. The rest of you, go back and call off the search."

The two grooms followed him to the tower, leading a horse behind them. Miss Sommersby was placed on the horse, brought back to the circle and then transferred to the carriage. With no spare horses, Freddie was forced to ride in the carriage with her. The trip back to the hall was made in nearly complete silence.

It was nearly midmorning when they returned home. Miss Sommersby still being unable to walk, Freddie summoned a footman to carry the girl inside. He followed along behind her.

As soon as they entered the house; they were immediately surrounded. Besides the servants, he saw his mother, his sister Priscilla and Miss Sommersby's parents.

"Freddie!" Priscilla exclaimed, wrapping him in a quick embrace. "I was afraid something perfectly dreadful had happened."

He gently untangled Priscilla's arms from around his neck. "As you see we are fine, although somewhat worse for the wear."

"Oh, my poor, poor, lamb. My poor dear," Mrs. Sommersby said, clucking over her daughter.

"George, we need to have a discussion," his mother said.

Now? She couldn't be serious. "Certainly," he said. "Once I have bathed and changed."

"There is no time for that," Lady Frederick snapped.

He could feel the trap closing in on him.

"We need to settle this, at once," Mr. Sommersby said.

"I am at your disposal," Freddie responded. "But perhaps Miss Sommersby will be more comfortable resting in her room until the physician arrives?"

"Yes, please," Miss Sommersby said.

"No, puss. This concerns you too," her father declared.

Every bone in Freddie's body ached with exhaustion. He was not ready for this confrontation. But there was no putting it off.

He nodded.

His mother turned and led the way to the nearest salon, followed by Mr. and Mrs. Sommersby. The footman carrying Miss Sommersby came next, followed by Freddie and lastly by Priscilla.

Freddie paused for a moment in the hall. "Prissy," he said, reverting to her childhood nickname, "what happened?"

For once his sister looked serious and wise beyond her years. "It was the most awful thing," she said. "When we came back to the clearing, you were nowhere in sight, and Ajax was gone. I thought you must have decided to ride home with Mama. So we left. It wasn't till we all met up at home that we realized you weren't with either party. By then, it was raining and nearly dark. Mr. Sommersby wanted to send servants out looking for you, but Mama said they would never find you in the storm. Mrs. Sommersby fainted, and Mr. Sommersby swore and called you all sorts of names."

He nodded. It made sense, if one didn't question how Ajax had managed to free himself from his hobbles and wander off. Nor did it explain why his mother had told everyone Miss Sommersby was leaving and then had let the girl wander off to pick flowers. But all he had were vague suspicions. And they did not erase the fact that he had spent the night with an unmarried young woman.

"You're going to have to marry her, aren't you?" Priscilla asked.

"It looks that way."

"This is all my fault. I wish I had never invited her."

He put a hand on her shoulder and gave it a comforting squeeze. But there was nothing he could say. Mere wishes would not change what had happened.

Freddie started toward the parlor. When Priscilla made to follow, he shooed her away. "Go. There is no need for you to witness this."

As he entered the room, he found himself the focus of all eyes.

Miss Sommersby reclined on a sofa, her wounded ankle propped up on a pillow. Her mother sat by her side, holding her daughter's hand. Lady Frederick sat across from Miss Sommersby, while Mr. Sommersby, the outraged father, had chosen to stand.

"So, young man," he said, "would you like to explain how it is that you came to treat my daughter in such a disgraceful fashion?"

Freddie's back stiffened. He had done nothing disgraceful. On the contrary, he had behaved as a perfect gentleman. And he had never taken kindly to being patronized. "Perhaps your daughter would like to explain why she took it into her head to wander off into the woods so that she had to be rescued?"

Mr. Sommersby's eyes turned to his daughter.

"I was lost, Papa," Miss Sommersby said, dabbing her eyes with a lace handkerchief. "And then I fell and twisted my ankle. Lord Frederick found me, and he would have brought me back, I am sure, but, well, the rain started, and then . . ."

It was a performance worthy of Drury Lane.

"What your daughter is trying to explain is that we sought shelter in the ruined tower until the storm had passed, and were forced to spend the night. I give you my word that nothing passed between us. I behaved as a perfect gentleman."

"Well, that is neither here nor there," Mr. Sommersby blustered. "What matters is what people will say once they hear my daughter has spent the night with a rake like you."

"I have been called many things before. But never a rake," Freddie said with quiet determination.

"Of course you behaved with honor. You are my son, after all," Lady Frederick said. "Still, there are appearances to be considered. There is only one thing you can do. You and Miss Sommersby must be wed."

"Indeed. It is the least you can do for my poor girl," her father said, then spoiled the effect by rubbing his hands together as if well pleased by this turn of events.

Ever since he had found Miss Sommersby in the ruins, Freddie had known that it would come to this. His mother was right. He was a gentleman, and as a gentleman it was left to him to do the honorable thing.

He opened his mouth to agree. But the word that he spoke was "No."

"No? What do you mean no?" Mr. Sommersby barked.

"No," Freddie said, relishing the taste of the word on his tongue. "I will not marry your daughter."

He could not have shocked them more if he had announced that he was a murderer.

"But you must," Mrs. Sommersby said.

"If this is a jest, it is a poor one," Lady Frederick said. "Of course you will marry Miss Sommersby."

He felt a strange reckless pleasure as he realized that he meant what he said. For once in his life he would choose happiness over duty, and be damned to the consequences.

He looked over at Miss Sommersby. "I am sorry, Miss Sommersby, but I do not think we will suit, and I will not be forced into marriage. I can live down a little scandal. Can you?"

Miss Sommersby sat bolt upright. "But you must marry me," she said. "Your mother said you would."

"My mother does not rule my life. I will stand by any story you care to tell, challenge anyone who dares slur your reputation. But I can not—I will not—marry you."

She blinked uncertainly at him. "You, you utter

beast!" she exclaimed. Then she jumped up and ran from the room.

Freddie watched her depart. "I see Miss Sommersby's ankle has made a miraculous recovery," he observed dryly.

Mr. Sommersby was taken aback, but only for a moment. "Now, sir, don't think I will let you get away with this—"

"Nor will I let Miss Sommersby trap me into marriage. For it seems to me that this was, indeed, not the accident it first appeared," Freddie said, giving his mother a hard glance. Under his scrutiny his mother flushed. "I thought as much."

Rage washed over him as he realized how close he had come to letting them ruin his life. And as quickly as the rage came, it passed, leaving him feeling wearier than ever.

He turned his attention back to the Sommersbys. "I take my leave of you. I will say nothing about these events, but I expect you and your daughter to be gone from this house before the sun sets."

And with that he turned on his heel and left.

The morning after Anne returned from Plymouth, she sent a note to Freddie asking that he call on her at his earliest convenience. Much to her surprise, she found that he had taken her at her word, and when the footman returned to the Manor Freddie accompanied him.

As Freddie entered her sitting room, she could see at once that he had been under some type of strain. There were lines of tiredness on his face, and his eyes sparkled brightly with fever or excitement.

"Freddie, is something wrong?"

"Yes," he replied. "I have been hopelessly compromised. According to my mother, I will shortly become an outcast from polite society," he said with a laugh.

"You are jesting," she accused.

"No, I mean it in all seriousness. Miss Sommersby, with, I suspect, the connivance of my mother, managed to lure me into a compromising position. You can imagine their surprise when I spoiled their plans by refusing to marry the chit."

Her heart, which had stopped for a moment at the mention of Miss Sommersby, began to beat again. Could this really be true? "But how? And why?" She had never known Freddie to refuse to do the honorable thing.

"Because I love you," he said simply. "And I was not about to let them ruin our lives."

She did not know what to say.

Freddie ran one hand through his hair. "Damn it, I meant to do better than this. It must be the lack of sleep has fuzzed my brain."

He crossed the few feet that separated them, and bent down on one knee before her. Taking her right hand between his, he said, "Anne, I can never give you up. I did not know what you meant to me until you were gone. These last six years I have been a sleepwalker, passing through life but never touching it. When I found you again, it was like finding a piece of my soul that I had thought lost forever."

He tipped his head up so he was looking straight into her eyes. "Say you will marry me. I will do whatever you want. I will claim Ian as my own. If you ask, I will go off with you to Canada and make a new life as a fur-trader. I will do anything you ask if only you promise that you will be mine."

It was an impassioned and utterly impractical proposal. And yet there was no doubt that he was sincere in his declaration of love. He had told her how much he loved Beechwood Park and how he could never imagine living anywhere else, but here he was, offering to give up everything for her.

Anne's heart felt as if it would burst. A smile split her face in two. "Stand up, you foolish man," she said.

"Not until you say yes."

"Yes," she replied. "Now stand up and kiss me."

He rose with alacrity and kissed her with a thoroughness that both shocked and delighted her. When he finally lifted his head, they were both breathless.

"Oh, my," she said.

"Oh, my," he echoed, giving her a look that heated her blood and made her heart race.

He gave a crooked smile. "So what is it to be? Will you be Viscountess Frederick? Or should I start packing for Canada?"

She knew, in the part of her that had always known him, that he would do whatever she asked. She did not know what she had done to deserve such a good man, and vowed that she would spend the rest of her life making him happy.

"I love you," she declared. "And I love your kindness in offering to go to Canada. But, if you are willing to endure the scandal that will result, I choose to stay."

"It will be a nine days' wonder, if that," Freddie said. "But my friends will stand by us, as will Elizabeth and the rest of my sisters. And as for my mother, it seems she has developed a sudden urge to travel abroad. I believe Italy was mentioned."

"I am sorry," Anne said, knowing that his mother's rejection must have hurt Freddie.

He shrugged his shoulders. "In time, she will come around."

"There is one thing more I should tell you," Anne said. "When I left here, I went to see Sarah's lover, Captain Montgomery."

Freddie nodded, but did not release her from his arms. "I had guessed as much," he said.

"Captain Montgomery never knew that Sarah was pregnant. He only learned of Ian's existence by accident and had called here to see if he could learn any news of the boy. His wife can not have children, so they asked to raise Ian as their own. Of course I refused, however I did agree to tell Ian about his father, and to let Ian visit with the Montgomerys from time to time." The words came out of her in a rush.

"Why did you not tell me?" he asked. "You can not imagine how worried I was when you disappeared without a word." He had imagined all sorts of dreadful things, including the possibility that Anne had run off with the captain. Only his faith in her had seen him through these last days.

"I wanted to. But I felt I had to make this decision as my own," she answered.

He nodded, his eyes full of understanding. He drew her back in his arms, and she rested her head against his chest, while he stroked her hair.

"Mama?"

She lifted her head and saw Ian standing in the

doorway. "Mama, why is Lord Frederick hugging you?"

"Because we are to be married," Freddie said firmly. He relinquished his hold on her and turned to face the child. "That is, if you agree?"

"I do," Ian said, nodding his head firmly. "I like you because you make Mama smile."

Anne blinked back the start of tears.

"Does this mean that you will be my father?" Ian asked.

"In a way, yes," Freddie replied.

Ian turned to Anne. "And Captain Montgomery, he is my father, too?"

"Yes," Anne answered. "But you will live with us."

Ian grinned, from ear to ear. "Two papas! I'll bet I'm the first boy to ever have two papas! I must go tell Sammy," he declared, and then dashed off.

"Will he be gone for long?" Freddie asked.

"Probably not," Anne replied. "So if you want to kiss me, you had better do so now. We are not likely to get this much privacy again till the wedding night."

He smiled uncertainly, as if unused to being the object of such affection. So she reached up and pulled his head down to hers. He might have much to teach her about making love, but she already knew all she needed to show him how much she loved him in return.

ABOUT THE AUTHOR

Patricia Bray is the author of two Zebra Regency romances: *A London Season* and *An Unlikely Alliance*. She is currently working on her fourth, *The Irish Earl*, which will be published in March, 2000. She loves to hear from her readers and you may write to her at: P.O. Box 273, Endicott, NY, 13761-0273. Please include a self-addressed stamped envelope if you wish a reply.

Put a Little Romance in Your Life With
Fern Michaels

__Dear Emily	0-8217-5676-1	$6.99US/$8.50CAN
__Sara's Song	0-8217-5856-X	$6.99US/$8.50CAN
__Wish List	0-8217-5228-6	$6.99US/$7.99CAN
__Vegas Rich	0-8217-5594-3	$6.99US/$8.50CAN
__Vegas Heat	0-8217-5758-X	$6.99US/$8.50CAN
__Vegas Sunrise	1-55817-5983-3	$6.99US/$8.50CAN
__Whitefire	0-8217-5638-9	$6.99US/$8.50CAN

Call toll free **1-888-345-BOOK** to order by phone or use this coupon to order by mail.

Name_____

Address_____

City _____ State _____Zip_____

Please send me the books I have checked above.

I am enclosing $_____

Plus postage and handling* $_____

Sales tax (in New York and Tennessee) $_____

Total amount enclosed $_____

*Add $2.50 for the first book and $.50 for each additional book.

Send check or money order (no cash or CODs) to:

Kensington Publishing Corp., 850 Third Avenue, New York, NY 10022

Prices and Numbers subject to change without notice.

All orders subject to availability.

Check out our website at **www.kensingtonbooks.com**

Put a Little Romance in Your Life With
Janelle Taylor

More Zebra Regency Romances

Put a Little Romance in Your Life With
Hannah Howell

__**My Valiant Knight** 0-8217-5186-7	**$5.50**US/**$7.00**CAN
__**Only For You** 0-8217-5943-4	**$5.99**US/**$7.50**CAN
__**Unconquered** 0-8217-5417-3	**$5.99**US/**$7.50**CAN
__**Wild Roses** 0-8217-5677-X	**$5.99**US/**$7.50**CAN
__**Highland Destiny** 0-8217-5921-3	**$5.99**US/**$7.50**CAN
__**Highland Honor** 0-8217-6095-5	**$5.99**US/**$7.50**CAN
__**A Taste of Fire** 0-8217-5804-7	**$5.99**US/**$7.50**CAN